Orsinian Tales

Books by Ursula K. Le Guin

NOVELS:

Rocannon's World
Planet of Exile
City of Illusions
The Left Hand of Darkness
A Wizard of Earthsea
The Tombs of Atuan
The Farthest Shore
The Lathe of Heaven
The Dispossessed

SHORT STORIES:

The Wind's Twelve Quarters
Orsinian Tales

POETRY:

Wild Angels

Orsinian Tales

Ursula K. Le Guin

Harper & Row, Publishers
New York, Hagerstown, San Francisco, London

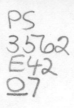

PS
3562
E42
O7

Grateful acknowledgment is made for permission to reprint the following:

"The Barrow" first appeared in *The Magazine of Fantasy and Science Fiction*, October 1976.

"Brothers and Sisters" first appeared in *The Little Magazine*, Vol. 10, Nos. 1 & 2, Summer 1976.

"A Week in the Country" first appeared in *The Little Magazine*, Vol. 9, No. 4, Spring 1976.

"An die Musik" first appeared in *The Western Humanities Review*, Vol. XV, No. 3, Summer 1961.

"Imaginary Countries" first appeared in *The Harvard Advocate*.

Designed by Gloria Adelson

Library of Congress Cataloging in Publication Data

Le Guin, Ursula K, date
    Orsinian tales.

    CONTENTS: The fountains, 1960.—The barrow,
1150.—Ile forest, 1902.—Conservations at night,
1920.—The road east, 1956. [etc.]
    I. Title
PZ4.L5180r   [PS3562.E42]   813'.5'4   76-5545
ISBN 0-06-012561-6

76 77 78 79 80 10 9 8 7 6 5 4 3 2

Contents

Orsinian Tales

The Fountains

THEY KNEW, having given him cause, that Dr Kereth might attempt to seek political asylum in Paris. Therefore, on the plane flying west, in the hotel, on the streets, at the meetings, even while he read his paper to the Cytology section, he was distantly accompanied at all times by obscure figures who might be explained as graduate students or Croatian microbiologists, but who had no names, or faces. Since his presence lent not only distinction to his country's delegation but also a certain luster to his government—See, we let even him come—they had wanted him there; but they kept him in sight. He was used to being in sight. In his small country a man could get out of sight only by not moving at all, by keeping voice, body, brain all quiet. He had always been a restless, visible man. Thus when all at once on the sixth day in the middle of a guided tour in broad daylight he found himself gone, he was confused for a time. Only by walking down a path could one achieve one's absence?

It was in a very strange place that he did so. A great, desolate, terrible house stood behind him yellow in the yellow sunlight of afternoon. Thousands of many-colored dwarfs milled on terraces, beyond which a pale blue canal ran straight away into the unreal distance of September. The lawns ended in groves of chestnut trees a hundred feet high, noble, somber, shot through with gold. Under the trees they had walked in shadow on the riding-paths of dead kings, but the guide led them out again to sunlight on lawns and marble pavements. And ahead, straight ahead, towering and shining up into the air, fountains ran.

They sprang and sang high above their marble basins in the light. The petty, pretty rooms of the palace as big as a city where no one lived, the indifference of the noble trees that were the only fit inhabitants of a garden too large for men, the dominance of autumn and the past, all this was brought into proportion by the running of water. The phonograph voices of the guides fell silent, the camera eyes of the guided saw. The fountains leapt up, crashed down exulting, and washed death away.

They ran for forty minutes. Then they ceased. Only kings could afford to run the Great Fountains of Versailles and live forever. Republics must keep their own proportion. So the high white jets shrank, stuttering. The breasts of nymphs ran dry, the mouths of river-gods gaped black. The tremendous voice of uprushing and downfalling water became a rattling, coughing sigh. It was all through, and everyone stood for a moment alone. Adam Kereth turned, and seeing a path before him went down it away from the marble terraces, under the trees. Nobody followed him; and it was at this moment, though he was unaware of it, that he defected.

Late-afternoon light lay warm across the path between shadows, and through the light and shadows a young man and a young woman walked hand in hand. A long way behind them Adam Kereth walked by himself, tears running down his cheeks.

Presently the shadows fell away from him and he looked up to see no path, no lovers, only a vast tender light and, below him, many little round trees in tubs. He had come to the terrace above the Orangerie. Southward from this high place one saw only forest, France a broad forest in the autumn evening. Horns blew no longer, rousing wolf or wild boar for the king's hunt; there was no great game left. The only tracks in that forest would be the footprints of young lovers who had come out from Paris on the bus, and walked among the trees, and vanished.

With no intent, unconscious still of his defection, Kereth roamed back along wide walks towards the palace, which stood now in the sinking light no longer yellow but colorless, like a sea-cliff over a beach when the last bathers are leaving. From beyond it came a dim roar like surf, engines of tourist busses starting back to Paris. Kereth stood still. A few small figures hurried on the terraces between silent fountains. A woman's voice far off called to a child, plaintive as a gull's cry. Kereth turned around and without looking back, intent now, conscious, erect as one who has just stolen something—a pineapple, a purse, a loaf—from a counter and has got it hidden under his coat, he strode back into the dusk among the trees.

"This is mine," he said aloud to the high chestnuts and the oaks, like a thief among policemen. "This is mine!" The oaks and chestnuts, French, planted for aristocrats, did not answer his fierce republican claim made in a foreign language. But all the same their darkness, the taciturn, complicit darkness of all forests where fugitives have hidden, gathered around him.

He was not long in the groves, an hour or less; there were gates to be locked and he did not want to be locked in. That was not what he was here for. So before nightfall he came up the terraces, still walking erect and calm as any king or kleptomaniac, and went around the huge, pale, many-windowed sea-cliff and across its cobbled beach. One bus still chuffed there, a blue bus, not the grey one he dreaded. His bus was gone. Gone, washed out to sea, with the guide, the colleagues, the fellow countrymen, the microbiologists, the spies. Gone and left him in possession of Versailles. Above him Louis XIV, foreshortened on a prodigious horse, asserted the existence of absolute privilege. Kereth looked up at the bronze face, the big bronze Bourbon nose, as a child looks up at his older brother, loving and derisive. He went on through the gates, and in a café across the Paris road his sister served him vermouth at a dusty green table under sycamores. The wind of night and autumn blew from the south, from the forests, and like the vermouth its scent was a little bitter, an odor of dry leaves.

A free man, he took his own way in his own time to the suburban station, bought his own ticket, returned to Paris by himself. Where he came up out of the Metro nobody knows, perhaps not himself, nor where he wandered in the city while defecting. At eleven o'clock at night he was standing at the parapet of the Solferino Bridge, a short man of forty-seven in a shoddy suit, a free man. He watched the lights of the bridge and of farther bridges tremble on the black river running quietly. Up and down the river on either bank stood the asylums: the Goverment of France, the Embassies of America and England. He had walked past them all. Perhaps it was too late at night to enter them. Standing on the bridge there in the middle, between the Left Bank and the Right Bank, he thought: There are no hiding places left. There are no thrones; no wolves, no boars; even the lions of Africa are dying out. The only safe place is the zoo.

But he had never cared much about being safe, and now thought that he did not care much about hiding either, having found something better: his family, his inheritance. Here he had at last walked in the garden larger than life, on paths where his older brothers had gone before him, crowned. After that he really could not take refuge in the zoo. He went on across the bridge and under the dark arches of the Louvre, returning to his hotel. Knowing now that he was both a king and a thief and so was at home anywhere, what turned him to his own land was mere fidelity. For what else should move a man, these days? Kingly he strode past the secret-police agent in the hotel lobby, hiding under his coat the stolen, inexhaustible fountains.

1960

4

The Barrow

NIGHT CAME DOWN along the snowy road from the mountains. Darkness ate the village, the stone tower of Vermare Keep, the barrow by the road. Darkness stood in the corners of the rooms of the Keep, sat under the great table and on every rafter, waited behind the shoulders of each man at the hearth.

The guest sat in the best place, a corner seat projecting from one side of the twelve-foot fireplace. The host, Freyga, Lord of the Keep, Count of the Montayna, sat with everybody else on the hearthstones, though nearer the fire than some. Cross-legged, his big hands on his knees, he watched the fire steadily. He was thinking of the worst hour he had known in his twenty-three years, a hunting trip, three autumns ago, to the mountain lake Malafrena. He thought of how the thin barbarian arrow had stuck up straight from his father's throat; he remembered how the cold mud had oozed against his knees as he knelt by his father's body in the reeds, in the circle of the dark mountains. His father's hair had stirred a little in the lake-water. And there had been a strange taste in his own mouth, the taste of death, like licking bronze. He tasted bronze now. He listened for the women's voices in the room overhead.

The guest, a travelling priest, was talking about his travels. He came from Solariy, down in the southern plains. Even merchants had stone houses there, he said. Barons had palaces, and silver platters, and ate roast beef. Count Freyga's liege men and servants listened open-mouthed. Freyga, listening to make the minutes pass, scowled. The guest had already complained of the stables, of the cold, of mutton for breakfast dinner and supper, of the dilapidated condition of Vermare Chapel and the way Mass was said there—"Arianism!" he had muttered, sucking in his breath and crossing himself. He told old Father Egius that every soul in Vermare was damned: they had received heretical baptism. "Arianism, Arianism!" he shouted. Father Egius, cowering, thought Arianism was a devil and tried to explain that no one in his parish had ever been possessed, except one of the count's rams, who had one yellow eye and one blue one and had butted a pregnant girl so that she miscarried her child, but they had sprinkled holy water on the ram and it made no more trouble, indeed was a fine breeder, and the girl, who had been pregnant out of wedlock, had married a good peasant from Bara and borne him five little Christians, one a year. "Heresy, adultery, ignorance!" the foreign priest had railed. Now he prayed for twenty minutes before he ate his mutton, slaughtered, cooked, and served by the hands of heretics. What did he want? thought Freyga. Did he expect comfort, in winter? Did he think they were heathens, with his "Arianism"? No doubt he had never seen a heathen, the little, dark, terrible people of Malafrena and the farther hills. No doubt he had never had a pagan arrow shot at him. That would teach him the difference between heathens and Christian men, thought Freyga.

When the guest seemed to have finished boasting for the time being, Freyga spoke to a boy who lay beside him chin in hand: "Give us a song, Gilbert." The boy smiled and sat up, and began at once in a high, sweet voice:

> King Alexander forth he came,
> Armored in gold was Alexander,
> Golden his greaves and great helmet,
> His hauberk all of hammered gold.
> Clad in gold came the king,

> Christ he called on, crossing himself,
>   In the hills at evening.
> Forward the army of King Alexander
> Rode on their horses, a great host,
> Down to the plains of Persia
> To kill and conquer, they followed the King,
>   In the hills at evening.

The long chant droned on; Gilbert had begun in the middle and stopped in the middle, long before the death of Alexander "in the hills at evening." It did not matter; they all knew it from beginning to end.

"Why do you have the boy sing of pagan kings?" said the guest.

Freyga raised his head. "Alexander was a great king of Christendom."

"He was a Greek, a heathen idolator."

"No doubt you know the song differently than we do," Freyga said politely. "As we sing it, it says, 'Christ he called on, crossing himself.' "

Some of his men grinned.

"Maybe your servant would sing us a better song," Freyga added, for his politeness was genuine. And the priest's servant, without much urging, began to sing in a nasal voice a canticle about a saint who lived for twenty years in his father's house, unrecognised, fed on scraps. Freyga and his household listened in fascination. New songs rarely came their way. But the singer stopped short, interrupted by a strange, shrieking howl from somewhere outside the room. Freyga leapt to his feet, staring into the darkness of the hall. Then he saw that his men had not moved, that they sat silently looking up at him. Again the faint howl came from the room overhead. The young count sat down. "Finish your song," he said. The priest's servant gabbled out the rest of the song. Silence closed down upon its ending.

"Wind's coming up," a man said softly.

"An evil winter it's been."

"Snow to your thighs, coming through the pass from Malafrena yesterday."

"It's their doing."

"Who? The mountain folk?"

"Remember the gutted sheep we found last autumn? Kass said then it was an evil sign. They'd been killing to Odne, he meant."

"What else would it mean?"

"What are you talking about?" the foreign priest demanded.

"The mountain folk, Sir Priest. The heathen."

"What is Odne?"

A pause.

"What do you mean, killing to Odne?"

"Well, sir, maybe it's better not to talk about it."

"Why?"

"Well, sir, as you said of the singing, holy things are better, tonight." Kass the blacksmith spoke with dignity, only glancing up to indicate the room overhead; but another man, a young fellow with sores around his eyes, murmured, "The Barrow has ears, the Barrow hears. . . ."

"Barrow? That hillock by the road, you mean?"

Silence.

Freyga turned to face the priest. "They kill to Odne," he said in his soft voice, "on stones beside the barrows in the mountains. What's inside the barrows, no man knows."

"Poor heathen men, unholy men," old Father Egius murmured sorrowfully.

"The altarstone of our chapel came from the Barrow," said the boy Gilbert.

"What?"

"Shut your mouth," the blacksmith said. "He means, sir, that we took the top stone from the stones beside the Barrow, a big marble stone, Father Egius blessed it and there's no harm in it."

"A fine altarstone," Father Egius agreed, nodding and smiling, but on the end of his words another howl rang out from overhead. He bent his head and muttered prayers.

"You pray too," said Freyga, looking at the stranger. He ducked his head and began to mumble, glancing at Freyga now and then from the corner of his eye.

There was little warmth in the Keep except at the hearth, and dawn found most of them still there: Father Egius curled up like an aged dormouse in the rushes, the stranger slumped in his chimney corner, hands clasped across his belly, Freyga sprawled out on his back like a man cut down in battle. His men snored around him, started in their sleep, made unfinished gestures. Freyga woke first. He stepped over the sleeping bodies and climbed the stone stairs to the floor above. Ranni the midwife met him in the anteroom, where several girls and dogs were sleeping in a heap on a pile of sheepskins. "Not yet, count."

"But it's been two nights now—"

"Ah, she's hardly begun," the midwife said with contempt. "Has to rest, hasn't she?"

Freyga turned and went heavily down the twisted stairs. The woman's contempt weighed upon him. All the women, all yesterday; their faces were stern, preoccupied; they paid no attention to him. He was outside, out in the cold, insignificant. He could not do anything. He sat down at the oaken table and put his head in his hands, trying to think of Galla, his wife. She was seventeen; they had been married ten months. He thought of her round white belly. He tried to think of her face but there was nothing but the taste of bronze on his tongue. "Get me something to eat!" he shouted, bringing his fist down on the board, and the Tower Keep of Vermare woke with a jump from the grey paralysis of dawn. Boys ran about, dogs yelped, bellows roared in the kitchen, men stretched and spat by the fire. Freyga sat with his head buried in his hands.

The women came down, one or two at a time, to rest by the great hearth and have a bite of food. Their faces were stern. They spoke to each other, not to the men.

The snow had ceased and a wind blew from the mountains, piling snowdrifts against the walls and byres, a wind so cold it cut off breath in the throat like a knife.

"Why has God's word not been brought to these mountain folk of yours, these sacrificers of sheep?" That was the potbellied priest, speaking to Father Egius and the man with sores around his eyes, Stefan.

They hesitated, not sure what "sacrificers" meant.

"It's not just sheep they kill," said Father Egius, tentatively. Stefan smiled. "No, no, no," he said, shaking his head.

"What do you mean?" The stranger's voice was sharp, and Father Egius, cowering slightly, said, "They—they kill goats, too."

"Sheep or goats, what's that to me? Where do they come from, these pagans? Why are they permitted to live in a Christian land?"

"They've always lived here," the old priest said, puzzled.

"And you've never tried to bring the Holy Church among them?"

"Me?"

It was a good joke, the idea of the little old priest going up into the mountains; there was a good deal of laughter for quite a while. Father Egius, though without vanity, was perhaps a little hurt, for he finally said in a rather stiff tone, "They have their gods, sir."

"Their idols, their devils, their what do you call it—Odne!"

"Be quiet, priest," Freyga said suddenly. "Must you say that name? Do you know no prayers?"

After that the stranger was less haughty. Since the count had spoken harshly to him the charm of hospitality was broken, the faces that looked at him were hard. That night he was again given the corner seat by the fire, but he sat huddled up there, not spreading his knees to the warmth.

There was no singing at the hearth that night. The men talked low, silenced by Freyga's silence. The darkness waited at their shoulders. There was no sound but the howling of the wind outside the walls and the howling of the woman upstairs. She had been still all day, but now the hoarse, dull yell came again and again. It seemed impossible to Freyga that she could still cry out. She was thin and small, a girl, she could not carry so much pain in her. "What good are they, up there!" he broke out. His men looked at him, saying nothing. "Father Egius! There is some evil in this house."

"I can only pray, my son," the old man said, frightened.

"Then pray! At the altar!" He hurried Father Egius before him out into the black cold, across the courtyard where dry snow whirled invisible on the wind, to the chapel. After some while he returned alone. The old priest had promised to spend the night on his knees by the fire in his little cell behind the chapel. At the great hearth only the foreign priest was still awake. Freyga sat down on the hearthstone and for a long time said nothing.

The stranger looked up and winced, seeing the count's blue eyes staring straight at him.

"Why don't you sleep?"

"I'm not sleepy, count."

"It would be better if you slept."

The stranger blinked nervously, then closed his eyes and tried to look asleep. He peered now and then under half-closed lids at Freyga and tried to repeat, without moving his lips, a prayer to his patron saint.

To Freyga he looked like a fat black spider. Rays of darkness spread out from his body, enwebbing the room.

The wind was sinking, leaving silence, in which Freyga heard his wife moaning, a dry, weak sound.

The fire died down. Ropes and webs of darkness tangled thicker and thicker around the man-spider in the corner of the hearth. A tiny glitter showed under his brows. The lower part of his face moved a little. He was casting his spells deeper, deeper. The wind had fallen. There was no sound at all.

Freyga stood up. The priest looked up at the broad golden figure looming against darkness, and when Freyga said, "Come with me," he was too frightened to move. Freyga took his arm and pulled him up. "Count, count, what do you want?" he whispered, trying to free himself.

"Come with me," Freyga said, and led him over the stone floor, through darkness, to the door.

Freyga wore a sheepskin tunic; the priest only a woollen gown. "Count," he gasped, trotting beside Freyga across the court, "it's cold, a man could freeze to death, there might be wolves—"

Freyga shot the arm-thick bolts of the outer gates of the Keep and swung one portal open. "Go on," he said, gesturing with his sheathed sword.

The priest stopped short. "No," he said.

Freyga unsheathed his sword, a short, thick blade. Jabbing its point at the rump beneath the woollen gown, he drove the priest before him out the gate, down the village street, out onto the rising road that led to the mountains. They went slowly, for the snow was deep and their feet broke through its crust at each step. The air was perfectly still now, as if frozen. Freyga looked up at the sky. Overhead between high faint clouds stood the star-shape with a swordbelt of three bright stars. Some called the figure the Warrior, others called it the Silent One, Odne the Silent.

The priest muttered one prayer after another, a steady pattering mumble, drawing breath with a whistling sound. Once he stumbled and fell face down in the snow. Freyga pulled him to his feet. He looked up at the young man's face in the starlight, but said nothing. He shambled on, praying softly and steadily.

The tower and village of Vermare were dark behind them; around them were empty hills and plains of snow, pale in the starlight. Beside the road was a hillock, less than a man's height, grave-shaped. Beside it, bared of snow by the wind, stood a short thick pillar or altar built of uncut stones. Freyga took the priest's shoulder, forcing him off the road and to the altar beside the Barrow. "Count, count—" the priest gasped when Freyga seized his head and forced it back. His eyes looked white in the starlight, his mouth was open to scream, but the scream was only a bubbling wheeze as Freyga slit his throat.

Freyga forced the corpse to bend over the altar, and cut and tore the thick gown away till he could slash the belly open. Blood and entrails gushed out over the dry stones of the altar and smoked on the dry snow. The gutted corpse fell forward over the stones like an empty coat, the arms dangling.

The living man sank down on the thin, wind-scoured snow beside the Barrow, sword still in hand. The earth rocked and heaved, and voices went crying past him in the darkness.

When he lifted his head and looked about him everything had changed. The sky, starless, rose in a high pale vault. Hills and far mountains stood distinct, unshadowed. The shapeless corpse slumped over the altar was black, the snow at the foot of the Barrow was black, Freyga's hands and sword-blade were black. He tried to wash his hands with snow, and the sting of it woke him. He got up, his head swimming, and stumbled back to Vermare on numb legs. As he went he felt the west wind, soft and damp, rising with the day around him, bringing the thaw.

Ranni was standing by the great hearth while the boy Gilbert built up the fire. Her face was puffy and grey. She spoke to Freyga with a sneer: "Well, count, high time you're back!"

He stood breathing heavily, slack-faced, and did not speak.

"Come along, then," said the midwife. He followed her up the twisting stairs. The straw that had covered the floor was swept aside into the fireplace. Galla lay again in the wide box-like bed, the marriage bed. Her closed eyes were deep-sunken. She was snoring faintly. "Shh!" the midwife said, as he started to her. "Be quiet! Look here."

She was holding up a tightly wrapped bundle.

After some while, as he still said nothing, she whispered sharply, "A boy. Fine, big."

Freyga put out one hand towards the bundle. His fingernails were caked and checked with brown.

The midwife drew the bundle closer to herself. "You're cold," she said in the sharp, contemptuous whisper. "Here." She drew back a fold to show for a moment a very tiny, purplish human face in the bundle, then rewrapped it.

Freyga went to the foot of the bed and knelt on the floor there, bending till his head was on the stones of the floor. He murmured, "Lord Christ, be praised, be thanked. . . ."

The Bishop of Solariy never found out what had become of his envoy to the northwest. Probably, being a zealous man, he had ventured too far into the mountains where heathen folk still lived, and had suffered martyrdom.

Count Freyga's name lived long in the history of his province. During his lifetime the Benedictine monastery on the mountain above Lake Malafrena was established. Count Freyga's flocks and

Count Freyga's sword fed and defended the monks in their first hard winters there. In the bad Latin of their chronicles, in black ink on the lasting vellum, he and his son after him are named with gratitude, staunch defenders of the Church of God.

1150

Ile Forest

"Surely," said the young doctor, "there are unpardonable crimes! Murder can't go unpunished."

The senior partner shook his head. "There are unpardonable people, perhaps; but crimes . . . they depend . . ."

"On what? To take a human life—that's absolute. Self-defense aside, of course. The sacredness of human life—"

"Is nothing the law can judge of," the older man said drily. "I have a murder in the family, as a matter of fact. Two murders." And, gazing mostly at the fire, he told his story.

My first practice was up north in the Valone. I went there with my sister in 1902. Even then it was a drab place. The old estates had sold out to the beetroot plantations, and collieries spread a murk on the hills to the south and west. It was just a big, dull plain; only at the east end of it, Valone Alte, did you get any sense of being in the mountains. On the first day I drove to Valone Alte I noticed a grove of trees; the trees in the valley had all been cut down. There were birches turning gold, and a house behind them, and behind it a stand of huge old oaks, turning dim red and brown; it was October. It was beautiful. When my sister and I drove out on Sunday I went that way, and she said in her drowsy way that it was like the castle in the fairy tale, the castle of silver in a forest of gold. I had several patients in Valone Alte, and always drove that road. In winter when the leaves were down you could see the old house; in spring you could hear the cuckoos calling, and in summer the mourning-doves. I didn't know if anyone lived there. I never asked.

The year went round; I didn't have all the practice I'd hoped for, but Poma, my sister Pomona, was good at making ends meet, for all she looked so sleepy and serene. So we got on. One evening I came in and found a call had been left from a place called Ile on the Valone Alte road. I asked Minna, the housekeeper, where it was.

"Why, in Ile Forest," she said, as if there was a forest the size of Siberia there. "Past the old mill."

"The castle of silver," Poma said, smiling. I set right off. I was curious. You know how it is, when you've built up your fancies about a place, and then suddenly are called to go into it. The old trees stood round, the windows of the house reflected the last red of the west. As I tied up my horse, a man came out to meet me.

He didn't come out of any fairy tale. He was about forty and had that hatchet face you see up north, hard as flint. He took me straight in. The house was unlit; he carried a kerosene lamp. What I could see of the rooms looked bare, empty. No carpets, nothing. The upstairs room we came to had no rug either; bed, table, a few chairs; but a roaring hot fire in the hearth. It helps to have a forest, when you need firewood.

The patient was the owner of the forest, Ileskar. Pneumonia. And he was a fighter. I was there on and off for seventy hours, and he never drew a breath in all that time that wasn't an act of pure willpower. The third night, I had a woman in labor in Mesoval, but I left her to the midwife. I was young, you know, and I said to myself that babies come into the world every day, but it's not every day a brave man leaves it. He fought; and I tried to help him. At dawn the fever went down abruptly, the way it does now with these new drugs, but it wasn't any drug; he'd fought, and won. I drove home in a kind of exaltation, in a white windy sunrise.

And I dropped in daily while he convalesced. He drew me, the place drew me. That last night, it had been one of those nights you have only when you're young—whole nights, from sunset to sunrise, when life and death are present with you, and outside the windows there's the forest, and the winter, and the dark.

I say "forest" just as Minna did, meaning that stand of a few hundred trees. It had been a forest once. It had covered all Valone Alte, and so had the Ileskar properties. For a century and a half it had all gone down and down; nothing left now but the grove, and the house, and a share in the Kravay plantations, enough to keep one Ileskar alive. And Martin, the hatchet-faced fellow, his servant technically, though they shared the work and ate together. Martin was a strange fellow, jealous, devoted to Ileskar. I felt that devotion as an actual force, not sexual, but possessive, defensive. It did not puzzle me too much. There was something about Galven Ileskar that made it seem quite natural. Natural to admire him, and to protect him.

I got his story from Minna, mostly; her mother had worked for his mother. The father had spent what was left to spend, and then died of the pleurisy. Galven went into the army at twenty; at thirty he married, retired as a captain, and came back to Ile. After about three years his wife deserted him, ran away with a man from Brailava. And about that I learned a little from Galven himself. He was grateful to me for my visits; I suppose it was plain that I wanted his friendship. He felt he should not withhold himself. I'd rambled on about Poma and myself, so he felt obliged to tell me about his marriage. "She was very weak," he said. He had a gentle, husky voice. "I took her weakness for sweetness. A mistake. But it wasn't her fault. A mistake. You know she left me, with another man."

I nodded, very embarrassed.

"I saw him whip a horse blind once," Galven said, in the same thoughtful, painful way. "Stand and whip its eyes till they were open sores. When I got there he'd just finished. He gave a big sigh of satisfaction, as if he'd just gotten up from dinner. It was his own horse. I didn't do anything. Told him to get off the place, clear out. Not enough. . . ."

"You and your—wife are divorced, then?"

"Yes," he said, and then he looked across the room at Martin, who was building up the fire. Martin nodded, and Galven said, "Yes," again. He was only a week or so convalescent, he looked tired; it was a bit strange, but I already knew he was a strange fellow. He said, "I'm sorry. I've forgotten how to talk to civilised people."

It was really painful to have him apologising to me, and so I just went on with the first thing that came to mind about Poma and myself and old Minna and my patients, and presently I wound up asking if I might bring Poma sometime when I came out to Ile. "She's admired the place so much when we drive past."

"It would be a great pleasure to me," Galven said. "But you'll let me get on my feet again, first? And it is a bit of a wolf's den, you know. . . ."

I was deaf. "She wouldn't notice that," I said. "Her own room's like a thicket, scarves and shawls and little bottles and books and hairpins, she never puts anything away. She never gets her buttons into the right buttonholes, and she leaves everything around behind her, sort of like a ship's wake." I wasn't exaggerating. Poma loved soft clothes and gauzy things, and wherever she'd been there was a veil dripping off a chair-arm, or a scarf fluttering on a rose bush, or some creamy fluffy thing dropped by the door, as if she were some sort of little animal that left bits of its fur around, the way rabbits leave white plumes on the briars in the early morning in the fields. When she'd lost a scarf and left her neck bare she'd catch up any sort of kerchief, and I'd ask her what she had on her shoulders now, the hearth-rug? and she'd smile her sweet, embarrassed, lazy smile. She was a sweet one, my little sister. I got a bit of a shock when I told her I'd take her out to Ile one of these days. "No," she said, like that.

"Why not?" I was chagrined. I'd talked a lot about Ileskar, and she had seemed interested.

"He doesn't want women and strangers around," she said. "Let the poor fellow be."

"Nonsense. He's very lonely, and doesn't know how to break out of it."

"Then you're just what he needs," she said, with a smile. I insisted—I was bent on doing Galven good, you see—and finally she said, "I have queer ideas about that place, Gil. When you talk about him, I keep thinking of the forest. The old forest, I mean, the way it must have been. A great, dim place, with glades no one ever sees, and places people have known but forgotten, and wild animals roaming in it. A place you get lost in. I think I'll stay home and tend my roses."

I suppose I said something about "feminine illogic," and the rest. Anyhow, I trampled on, and she gave in to me. To yield was her grace, as not to yield was Galven's. No day had been set for our visit, and that reassured her. In fact it was a couple of months before she went to Ile.

I remember the wide, heavy, February sky hanging over the valley as we drove there. The house looked naked in that winter light among bare trees. You saw the shingles off the roof, the uncurtained windows, the weedy driveways. I had spent an uneasy night, dreaming that I was trying to track somebody, some little animal it seemed, through the woods, and never finding it.

Martin wasn't about. Galven put up our pony and brought us into the house. He was wearing old officer's trousers with the stripe taken off, an old coat and a coarse woollen muffler. I had never noticed, till I looked through Poma's eyes, how poor he was. Compared with him, we were wealthy: we had our coats, our coals, our cart and pony, our little treasures and possessions. He had an empty house.

He or Martin had felled one of the oaks to feed the enormous fireplace downstairs. The chairs we sat in were from his room upstairs. We were cold, we were stiff. Galven's good manners were frozen. I asked where Martin was. "Hunting," Galven said, expressionless.

"Do you hunt, Mr Ileskar?" Poma asked. Her voice was easy, her face looked rosy in the firelight. Galven looked at her and thawed. "I used to go over to the marshes for duck, when my wife was alive," he said. "There aren't many birds left, but I liked it, wading out in the marshes as the sun came up."

"Just the thing for a bad chest," I said, "take it up again by all means." All at once we were all relaxed. Galven got to telling us hunting stories that had been passed down in his family—tales of boar-hunting; there'd been no wild boar in the Valone for a hundred years. And that sent us to the tales that old villagers like Minna could still tell you in those days; Poma was fascinated with them, and Galven told her one, a kind of crude, weird epic of avalanches and axe-armed heroes which must have come down from hut to hut, over the centuries, from the high mountains above the valley. He spoke well, in his dry, soft voice, and we listened well, there by the fire, with drafts and shadows at our back. I tried to write that tale down once, and found I could remember only fragments, all the poetry of it gone; but I heard Poma tell it to her children once, word for word as Galven told it that afternoon in Ile.

As we drove away from the place I thought I saw Martin come out of the forest towards the house, but it was too dark to be sure.

At supper Poma asked, "His wife is dead?"

"Divorced."

She poured some tea and dreamed over it awhile.

"Martin was avoiding us," I said.

"Disapproves of my coming there."

"He's a dour one all right. But you did like Galven?"

Poma nodded and presently, as if by afterthought, smiled. And soon she drifted off to her room, leaving a filmy pink scarf clinging to her chair by a thread.

After a few weeks Galven called on us. I was flattered, and startled. I had never imagined him away from Ile, standing like anybody else in our six-by-six parlour. He had got himself a horse, in Mesoval. He was tremendously pleased and serious, explaining to us how it was a really fine mare, but old and overridden, and how you went about "bringing back" a ruined horse. "When she's fit again, perhaps you'd like to ride her, Miss Pomona," he said, for my sister had mentioned that she loved riding. "She's very gentle."

Pomona accepted at once; she never could resist a ride—"It's my laziness," she always said, "the horse does the work, and I just sit there."

While Galven was there, Minna kept peering through the crack of the door. After he'd gone she treated us with the first inkling of respect she'd shown us yet. We'd moved up a notch in the world. I took advantage of it to ask her about the man from Brailava.

"He used to come to hunt. Mr Ileskar used to entertain, those days. Not like in his father's day, but still, there'd be ladies and gentlemen come. That one come for the hunting. They say he beat his horse blind and then had an awful quarrel with Mr Ileskar about it and was sent off. But he come back, I guess, and made a fool of Mr Ileskar after all."

So it was true about the horse. I hadn't been sure. Galven did not lie, but I had a notion that in his loneliness he had not kept a firm hold on the varieties, the distinctions, of truth. I don't know what gave me that impression, other than his having said once or twice that his wife was dead; and she was, for him, if not for others. At any rate Minna's grin displeased me—her silly respect for Ileskar as "a gentleman," and disrespect for him as a man. I said so. She shrugged her wide shoulders. "Well, doctor, then tell me why he didn't up and follow 'em? Why'd he let the fellow just walk off with his wife?"

She had a point there.

"She wasn't worth his chasing after," I said. Minna shrugged again, and no wonder. By her code, and Galven's, that was not how pride worked.

In fact it was inconceivable that he had simply given in. I had seen him fight a worse enemy than an adulterer. . . . Had Martin somehow interfered? Martin was a strong Christian; he had a different code. But strong as he might be he could not have held Galven back from anything Galven willed to do. It was all very curious, and I brooded over it at odd moments all that spring. It was the *passiveness* of Galven's behavior that I simply could not fit in to the proud, direct, intransigent man I thought I knew. Some step was missing.

I took Poma out several times to ride at Ile that spring; the winter had left her a bit run down, and I prescribed the exercise. That gave Galven great pleasure. It was a long time since he'd felt himself of use to another human being. Come June he got a second horse, when his money from the Kravay plantations came in; it was called Martin's horse, and Martin rode it when he went to Mesoval, but Galven rode it when Poma came to ride the old black mare. They were a funny pair, Galven every inch the cavalryman on the big rawboned roan, Poma lazy and smiling, sidesaddle on the fat old mare. All summer he'd ride down on Sunday afternoon leading the mare, pick up Poma, and they'd ride out all afternoon. She came in bright-eyed from these rides, wind-flushed, and I laid it to the outdoor exercise—oh, there's no fool like a young doctor!

There came an evening of August, the evening of a hot day. I'd been on an obstetrics call, five hours, premature twins, stillborn, and I came home about six and lay down in my room. I was worn out. The stillbirth, the sickly heavy heat, the sky grey with coal-smoke over the flat, dull plain, it all pulled me down. Lying there I heard horses' hooves on the road, soft on the dust, and after a while I heard Galven's and Pomona's voices. They were in the little rose plot under my window. She was saying, "I don't know, Galven."

"You cannot come there," he said.

If she answered, I could not hear her.

"When the roof leaks there," he said, "it leaks. We nail old shingles over the hole. It takes money to roof a house like that. I have no money. I have no profession. I was brought up not to have a profession. My kind of people have land, not money. I don't have land. I have an empty house. And it's where I live, it's what I am, Pomona. I can't leave it. But you can't live there. There is nothing there. Nothing."

"There's yourself," she said, or I think that's what she said; she spoke very low.

"It comes to the same thing."

"Why?"

There was a long pause. "I don't know," he said. "I started out all right. It was coming back, maybe. Bringing her back to that house. I tried it, I tried to give Ile to her. It is what I am. But it wasn't any good, it isn't any good, it's no use, Pomona!" That was said in anguish, and she answered only with his name. After that I couldn't hear what they said, only the murmur of their voices, unnerved and tender. Even in the shame of listening it was a wonderful thing to hear, that tenderness. And still I was afraid, I felt the sickness, the weariness I had felt that afternoon bringing the dead to birth. It was impossible that my sister should love Galven Ileskar. It wasn't that he was poor, it wasn't that he chose to live in a half-ruined house at the end of nowhere; that was his heritage, that was his right. Singular men lead singular lives. And Poma had the right to choose all that, if she loved him. It wasn't that that made it impossible. It was the missing step. It was something more profoundly lacking, lacking in Galven. There was a gap, a forgotten place, a break in his humanity. He was not quite my brother, as I had thought all men were. He was a stranger, from a different land.

That night I kept looking at Poma; she was a beautiful girl, as soft as sunlight. I damned myself for not ever having looked at her, for not having been a decent brother to her, taking her somewhere, anywhere, into company, where she'd have found a dozen men ready to love her and marry her. Instead, I had taken her to Ile.

"I've been thinking," I said next morning at breakfast. "I'm fed up with this place. I'm ready to try Brailava." I thought I was being subtle, till I saw the terror in her eyes.

"Are you?" she said weakly.

"All we'll ever do here is scrape by. It's not fair to you, Poma. I'm writing Cohen to ask him to look out for a partnership for me in the city."

"Shouldn't you wait a while longer?"

"Not here. It gets us nowhere."

She nodded, and left me as soon as she could. She didn't leave a scarf or handkerchief behind, not a trace. She hid in her room all day. I had only a couple of calls to make. God, that was a long day!

I was watering the roses after supper, and she came to me there, where she and Galven had talked the night before. "Gil," she said, "I want to talk with you."

"Your skirt's caught on the rose bush."

"Unhook me, I can't reach it."

I broke the thorn and freed her.

"I'm in love with Galven," she said.

"Oh I see," said I.

"We talked it over. He feels we can't marry; he's too poor. I wanted you to know about it, though. So you'd understand why I don't want to leave the Valone."

I was wordless, or rather words strangled me. Finally I got some out—"You mean you want to stay here, even though—?"

"Yes. At least I can see him."

She was awake, my sleeping beauty. He had waked her; he had given her what she lacked, and what few men could have given her: the sense of peril, which is the root of love. Now she needed what she had always had and never needed, her serenity, her strength. I stared at her and finally said, "You mean to live with him?"

She turned white, dead white. "I would if he asked me," she said. "Do you think he'd do that?" She was furious, and I was floored. I stood there with the watering can and apologised—"Poma, I'm sorry, I didn't mean to— But what are you going to do?"

"I don't know," she said, still angry.

"You mean you just intend to go on living here, and he there, and—" She already had me at the point of telling her to marry him. I got angry in my turn. "All right," I said, "I'll go speak to him."

"What about?" she said, defensive of him at once.

"About what he intends to do! If he wants to marry you, surely he can find some kind of work?"

"He has tried," she said. "He wasn't brought up to work. And he has been ill, you know."

Her dignity, her vulnerable dignity, went to my heart. "Oh Poma, I know that! And you know that I respect him, that I love him; he was my friend first, wasn't he? But the illness—what kind of illness?—There are times I don't think I've ever really known him at all—" I could not say any more, for she did not understand me. She was blind to the dark places in the forest, or they were all bright to her. She feared for him; but she did not fear him at all.

And so I rode off that evening to Ile.

Galven was not there. Martin said he had taken out the mare to exercise her. Martin was cleaning harness in the stable by lantern-light and moonlight, and I talked with him there while I waited for Galven to come back. Moonlight enlarged the woods of Ile; the birches and the house looked silver, the oaks were a wall of black. Martin came to the stable door with me for a smoke. I looked at his face in the moonlight, and I thought I could trust him, if only he'd trust me.

"Martin, I want to ask you something. I have good reason for asking it."

He sucked at his pipe, and waited.

"Do you consider Galven to be sane?"

He was silent; sucked at his pipe; grinned a little. "Sane?" he said. "I'm not one to judge. I chose to live here too."

"Listen, Martin, you know that I'm his friend. But he and my sister, they're in love, they talk of marrying. I'm the only one to look after her. I want to know more about—" I hesitated and finally said, "About his first marriage."

Martin was looking out into the yard, his light eyes full of moonlight. "No need to stir that up, doctor. But you ought to take your sister away."

"Why?"

No answer.

"I have a right to know."

"Look at him!" Martin broke out, fierce, turning on me. "Look at him! You know him well enough, though you'll never know what he was, what he should have been. What's done is done, there's no mending it, let him be. What would she do, here, when he went into his black mood? I've lived day after day in this house with him when he never spoke a word, and there was nothing you could do for him, nothing. Is that for a young girl to live with? He's not fit to live with people. He's not sane, if you want. Take her away from here!"

It was not wholly jealousy, but it was not logic, either, that led his argument. Galven had argued against himself in the same way last night. I was sure Galven had had no "black mood" since he had known Poma. The blackness lay further behind.

"Did he divorce his wife, Martin?"

"She's dead."

"You know that for a fact?"

Martin nodded.

"All right; if she's dead, that story's closed. All I can do is speak to him."

"You won't do that!"

It wasn't either question or threat so much as it was terror, real terror in his voice. I was clinging to common sense by now desperately, clutching at the straw. "Somebody's got to face reality," I said angrily. "If they marry they've got to have something to live on—"

"To live on, to live on, that's not what it's about! He can't marry anybody. Get her out of here!"

"Why?"

"All right, you asked if he was sane, I'll answer you. No. No, he isn't sane. He's done something he doesn't know about, he doesn't remember, if she comes here it will happen again, how do I know it won't happen again!"

I felt very dizzy, there in the night wind under the high dark and silver of the trees. I finally said in a whisper, "His wife?"

No answer.

"For the love of God, Martin!"

"All right," the man whispered. "Listen. He came on them in the woods. There, back in the oaks." He pointed to the great trees standing somber under moonlight. "He'd been out hunting. It was the day after he'd sent off the man from Brailava, told him get out and never come back. And she was in a rage with him for it, they'd quarrelled half the night, and he went off to the marshes before dawn. He came back early and he found them there, he took a short cut through the woods, he found them there in broad daylight in the forest. And he shot her point-blank and clubbed the man with his rifle, beat his brains out. I heard the shot, so close to the house, I came out and found them. I took him home. There were a couple of other men staying here, I sent them away, I told them she'd run off. That night he tried to kill himself, I had to watch him, I had to tie him up." Martin's voice shook and broke again and again. "For weeks he never said a word, he was like a dumb animal, I had to lock him in. And it wore off but it would come back on him, I had to watch him night and day. It wasn't her, it wasn't that he'd come on them that way like dogs in heat, it was that he'd killed them, that's what broke him. He came out of it, he began to act like himself again, but only when he'd forgotten that. He forgot it. He doesn't remember it. He doesn't know it. I told him the same story, they'd run off, gone abroad, and he believed it. He believes it now. Now, now will you bring your sister here?"

All I could say at first was, "Martin, I'm sorry, I'm sorry." Then, pulling myself together, "They—what did you do?"

"They're where they died. Do you want to dig them up and make sure?" he said in a cracked, savage voice. "There in the forest. Go ahead, here, here's the manure shovel, it's what I dug a hole for them with. You're a doctor, you won't believe Galven could do that to a man, there wasn't anything left of the head but —but—" Martin put his face into his hands suddenly and rocked back and forth, crouching down on his heels, crouching and rocking and sobbing.

I said what I could to him, but all he could say to me was, "If I could just forget it, the way he has!"

When he began to get himself under control again, I left, not waiting for Galven. Not waiting, I say—I was running from him. I wanted to be out from under the shadow of those trees. I kept the pony at a trot all the way home, glad of the empty road and the wash of moonlight over the wide valley. And I came into our house out of breath and shaking; and found Galven Ileskar standing there, by the fire, alone.

"Where's my sister?" I yelled, and he stared in bewilderment. "Upstairs," he stammered, and I went up the stairs four at a time. There she was in her room, sitting on her bed, among all the pretty odds and ends and bits and tatters that she never put away. She had been crying. "Gil!" she said, with the same bewildered look. "What's wrong?"

"Nothing—I don't know," and I backed out, leaving her scared to death, poor girl. But she waited up there while I came back down to Galven; that's what they'd arranged, the custom of the times, you know, the men were to talk the matter over.

He said the same thing: "What's wrong, Gil?" And what was I to say? There he stood, tense and gallant, with his clear eyes, my friend, ready to tell me he loved my sister and had found some kind of job and would stand by her all his life, and was I supposed to say, "Yes, there's something wrong, Galven Ileskar," and tell him what it was? Oh, there was something wrong, all right, but it was a deeper wrong, and an older one, than any he had done. Was I to give in to it?

"Galven, " I said, "Poma's spoken to me. I don't know what to say. I can't forbid you to marry, but I can't—I can't—" And I stuck; I couldn't speak; Martin's tears blinded me.

"Nothing could make me hurt her," he said very quietly, as if making a promise. I don't know whether he understood me; I don't know whether, as Martin believed, he did not know what he had done. In a way it did not matter. The pain and the guilt of it were in him, then and always. That he knew, knew from end to end, and endured without complaint.

Well, that wasn't quite the end of it. It should have been, but what he could endure, I couldn't, and finally, against every impulse of mercy, I told Poma what Martin had told me. I couldn't let her walk into the forest undefended. She listened to me, and as I spoke I knew I'd lost her. She believed me, all right. God help her, I think she knew before I told her!—not the facts, but the truth. But my telling her forced her to take sides. And she did. She said she'd stay with Ileskar. They were married in October.

The doctor cleared his throat, and gazed a long time at the fire, not noticing his junior partner's impatience.

"Well?" the young man burst out at last like a firecracker—"What happened?"

"What happened? Why, nothing much happened. They lived on at Ile. Galven had got himself a job as an overseer for Kravay; after a couple of years he did pretty well at it. They had a son and a daughter. Galven died when he was fifty; pneumonia again, his heart couldn't take it. My sister's still at Ile. I haven't seen her for a couple of years, I hope to spend Christmas there. . . . Oh, but the reason I told you all this. You said there are unpardonable crimes. And I agree that murder ought to be one. And yet, among all men, it was the murderer whom I loved, who turned out in fact to be my brother. . . . Do you see what I mean?"

1920

Conversations at Night

"The best thing to do is get him married."

"Married?"

"Shh."

"Who'd marry him?"

"Plenty of girls! He's still a big strong fellow, good-looking. Plenty of girls."

When their sweating arms or thighs touched under the sheet they moved apart with a jerk, then lay again staring at the dark.

"What about his pension?" Albrekt asked at last. "She'd get it."

"They'd stay here. Where else? Plenty of girls would jump at the chance. Rent-free. She'd help at the shop, and look after him. Fat chance I'd give up his pension after all I've done. Not even my blood kin. They'd have your brother's room, and he'd sleep in the hall."

This detail gave so much reality to the plan that only after a long time, during which he had scratched his sweaty arms to satisfaction, did Albrekt ask, "You think of anybody special?"

In the hall outside their door a bed creaked as the sleeper turned. Sara was silent a minute, then whispered, "Alitsia Benat."

"Huh!" Albrekt said in vague surprise. The silence lengthened, drew into uneasy, hot-weather sleep. Sara not knowing she had slept found herself sitting up, the sheet tangled about her legs. She got up and peered into the hall. Her nephew lay asleep; the skin of his bare arms and chest looked hard and pale, like stone, in the first light.

"Why'd you yell like that?"

He sat up suddenly, his eyes wide. "What is it?"

"You were talking, yelling. I need my sleep."

He lay still. After Sara had settled back into bed it was silent. He lay listening to the silence. At last something seemed to sigh deeply, outside, in the dawn. A breath of cooler air brushed over him. He also sighed; he turned over on his face and sank into sleep, which was a whiteness to him, like the whitening day.

Outside the dreams, outside the walls, the city Rákava stood still in daybreak. The streets, the old wall with its high gates and towers, the factories that bulked outside the wall, the gardens at the high south edge of town, the whole of the long, tilted plain on which the city was built, lay pale, drained, unmoving. A few fountains clattered in deserted squares. The west was still cold where the great plain sloped off into the dark. A long cloud slowly dissolved into a pinkish mist in the eastern sky, and then the sun's rim, like the lip of a cauldron of liquid steel, tipped over the edge of the world, pouring out daylight. The sky turned blue, the air was streaked with the shadows of towers. Women began to gather at the fountains. The streets darkened with people going to work; and then the rising and falling howl of the siren at the Ferman cloth-factory went over the city, drowning out the slow striking of the cathedral bell.

The door of the apartment slammed. Children were shrieking down in the courtyard. Sanzo sat up, sat on the edge of his bed for a while; after he had dressed he went into Albrekt and Sara's room and stood at the window. He could tell strong light from darkness, but the window faced the court and caught no sunlight. He stood with his hands on the sill, turning his head sometimes, trying to catch the contrast of dark and light, until he heard his father moving about and went into the kitchen to make the old man his coffee.

His aunt had not left the matches in their usual place to the left of the sink. He felt about for the tin box along the counter and shelf, his hands stiff with caution and frustration. He finally located it left out on the table, in plain sight, if he had been able to see. As he got the stove lighted his father came shuffling in.

"How goes it?" Sanzo said.

"The same, the same." The old man was silent till the coffee was ready, then said, "You pour, I got no grip this morning."

Sanzo located the cup with his left hand, brought the coffeepot over it with his right. "On the mark," Volf said, touching his son's hand with his rigid arthritic fingers to keep it in the right place. Between them they got their cups filled. They sat at the table in silence, the father chewing on a piece of bread.

"Hot again," he mumbled.

A bluebottle buzzed in the window, knocking against the glass. That sound and the sound of Volf chewing his bread filled Sanzo's world. A knock on the door came like a gunshot. He jumped up. The old man went on chewing.

He opened the door. "Who is it?" he said.

"Hullo, Sanzo. Lisha."

"Come on in."

"Here's the flour mother borrowed Sunday," she whispered.

"The coffee's hot."

The Benat family lived across the courtyard; Sanzo had known them all since he was ten, when he and his father had come to live with Albrekt and Sara. He had no clear picture of how Alitsia looked, having seen her last when she was fourteen. Her voice was soft, thin, and childish.

She still had not come in. He shrugged and held out his hands for the flour. She put the bag square in his hands so that he did not have to fumble for it.

"Oh, come on in," he said. "I never see you any more."

"Just for a minute. I have to get back to help mother."

"With the laundry? Thought you were working at Rebolts."

"They laid off sixty cutters at the end of last month."

She sat with them at the kitchen table. They talked about the proposed strike at the Ferman cloth-factory. Though Volf had not worked for five years, crippled by arthritis, he was full of information from his drinking-companions, and Lisha's father was a Union section-head. Sanzo said little. After a while there was a pause.

"Well, what do you see in him?" said the old man's voice.

Lisha's chair creaked; she said nothing.

"Look all you like," Sanzo said, "it's free." He stood up and felt for the cups and plates on the table.

"I'd better go."

"All right!" Turning towards the sink, he misjudged her position, and ran right into her. "Sorry," he said, angrily, for he hated to blunder. He felt her hand, just for a moment, laid very lightly on his arm; he felt the movement of her breath as she said, "Thanks for the coffee, Sanzo." He turned his back, setting the cups down in the sink.

She left, and Volf left a minute later, working his way down the four flights of stairs to the courtyard where he would sit most of the day, hobbling after the sunlight as it shifted from the west to the east wall, until the evening sirens howled and he went to meet his old companions, off work, at the corner tavern. Sanzo washed up the dishes and made the beds, then took his stick and went out. At the Veterans' Hospital they had taught him a blind-man's trade, chair-caning, and Sara had hunted and badgered the local used-furniture sellers until one of them agreed to give Sanzo what caning work came his way. Often it was nothing, but this week there was a set of eight chairs to be done. It was eleven blocks to the shop, but Sanzo knew his routes well. The work itself, in the silent room behind the shop, in the smell of newly cut cane, varnish, mildew, and glue, was pleasant, hypnotic; it was past four when he knocked off, bought himself a sausage roll at the corner bakery, and followed another leg of his route to his uncle's shop, CHEKEY: STATIONERS, a hole in the wall where they sold paper, ink, astrological charts, string, dream-books, pencils, tacks. He had been helping Albrekt, who had no head for figures, with the accounting. But there was very little accounting to be done these days; there were no customers in the shop, and he could hear Sara in the back room working herself up into a rage at Albrekt over something. He shut the shop door so the bell would jangle and bring her out to the front hoping for a customer, and strode on the third leg of his circuit, to the park.

It was fiercely hot, though the sun was getting lower. When he looked up at the sun, a greyish mist pressed on his eyes. He found his usual bench. Insects droned in the dry park grass, the city hummed heavily, voices passed by, near and far, in the void. When he felt the shadows rising up around him he started home. His head had begun to ache. A dog followed him for blocks. He could hear its panting and its nails scratching on the pavement. A couple of times he struck out at it with his stick, when he felt it crowding at his ankles, but he did not hit it.

After supper, eaten in haste and silence in the hot kitchen, he sat out in the courtyard with his father and uncle and Kass Benat. They spoke of the strike, of a new dyeing process that was going to cost a whole caste of workmen their jobs, of a foreman who had murdered his wife and children yesterday. The night was windless and sticky.

At ten they went to bed. Sanzo was tired but it was too hot, too close for sleep. He lay thinking again and again that he would get up and go down and sit in the courtyard where it would be cooler. There was a soft, interminable roll of thunder, seeming to die away then muttering on, louder then softer. The hot night gathered round him swathing him in sticky folds, pressing on him, as the girl's body had pressed on him for a second that morning when he had run against her. A sudden chill breeze whacked at the windows, the air changed, the thunder grew loud. Rain began to patter. Sanzo lay still. He knew by a greyish movement inside his eyes when the lightning flashed. Thunder echoed deafening in the well of the courtyard. The rain increased, rattling on the windows. As the storm slackened he relaxed; languor came into him, a faint, sweet well-being; without fear or shame he began to pursue the memory of that moment, that touch, and following it found sleep.

Sara had been polite to him for three days running. Distrustful, he sought to provoke her, but she saved her tantrums for Volf and

Albrekt, left the matches where Sanzo could find them, asked him if he didn't want a few kroner back from his pension so he could go to the tavern, and finally asked him if he wouldn't like somebody to come in and read to him now and then.

"Read what?"

"The newspaper, anything you like. It wouldn't be so dull for you. One of the Benat children would do it, Lisha maybe, she's always got a book. You used to read so much."

"I don't any more," he said with stupid sarcasm, but Sara sailed on, talking about Mrs Benat's laundry business, Lisha's losing her job, where Sanzo's mother's old books might have got to, she had been a great reader too, always with a book. Sanzo half listened, made no reply, and was not surprised when Lisha Benat turned up, late the next afternoon, to read to him. Sara usually got her way. She had even dug out, from the closet in Volf's room, three books that had belonged to Sanzo's mother, old novels in school editions. Lisha, who sounded very ill at ease, started in promptly to read one of them, Karantay's *The Young Man Liyve*. She was husky and fidgety at first, but then began to get interested in what she was reading. She left before Sara and Albrekt came home, saying, "Shall I come back tomorrow?"

"If you want," Sanzo said. "I like your voice."

By the third afternoon she was quite caught in the spell of the long, gentle, romantic story. Sanzo, bored and yet at peace, listened patiently. She came to read two or three afternoons a week, when her mother did not need her; he took to being at home by four, in case she came.

"You like that fellow Liyve," he said one day when she had closed the book. They sat at the kitchen table. It was close and quiet in the kitchen, evening of a long September day.

"Oh, he's so unhappy," she said with such compassion that she then laughed at herself. Sanzo smiled. His face, handsome and rigidly intent, was broken by the smile, changed, brought alive. He reached out, found the book and her hand on it, and put his own hand over hers. "Why does that make you like him?"

"I don't know!"

He got up abruptly and came round the table till he stood right by her chair, so that she could not get up. His face had returned to its usual intent look. "Is it dark?"

"No. Evening."

"I wish I could see you," he said, and his left hand groped and touched her face. She started at the very gentle touch, then sat motionless. He took her by the arms, a groping touch again but followed by a hard grip, and pulled her up to stand against him. He was shaking; she stood quiet in his arms, pressed against him. He kissed her mouth and face, his hand struggled with the buttons of her blouse; then abruptly he let her go, and turned away.

She caught a deep breath, like a sob. The faint September wind stirred around them, blowing in from the open window in another room. He still did not turn, and she said softly, "Sanzo—"

"You'd better go on," he said. "I don't know. Sorry. Go on, Lisha."

She stood a moment, then bent and put her lips against his hand, which rested on the table. She picked up her kerchief and went out. When she had closed the door behind her she stopped on the landing outside. There was no sound for some while, then she heard a chair scrape in the apartment, and then, so faint she was not certain it came from behind that door, a whistled tune. Somebody was coming up the stairs and she ran down, but the tune stayed in her head; she knew the words, it was an old song. She hummed it as she crossed the courtyard.

> Two tattered beggars met on the street,
> 'Hey, little brother, give me bread to eat!'

After two days she came again. Neither of them had much to say, and she set to reading at once. They had got to the chapter where the poet Liyve, ill in his garret, is visited by Countess Luisa, the chapter called "The First Night." Lisha's mouth was dry, and several times her breath stuck in her throat. "I need a drink of water," she said, but she did not get it. When she stood up he did, and when she saw him reach out his hand she took it.

This time in her acceptance of him there was one obscure moment, a movement suppressed before it was made, before she knew she had resisted anything. "All right," he whispered, and his hands grew gentler. Her eyes were closed, his were open; they stood there not in lamplight but in darkness, and alone.

The next day they had a go at reading, for they still could not talk to each other, but the reading ended sooner than before. Then for several days Lisha was needed in the laundry. As she worked she kept singing the little song.

> 'Go to the baker's house, ask him for the key,
> If he won't hand it over, say you were sent by me!'

Stooping over the laundry tub, her mother took up the song with her. Lisha stopped singing.

"Can't I sing it too, since I've got it in my ears all day?" Mrs Benat plunged her red, soap-slick arms into the steaming tub. Lisha cranked the wringer on a stiff pair of overalls.

"Take it easy. What's wrong?"

"They won't go through."

"Button caught, maybe. Why are you so jumpy lately?"

"I'm not."

"I'm not Sanzo Chekey, I can see you, my girl!"

Silence again, while Lisha struggled with the wringer. Mrs Benat lifted a basket of wet clothes to the table, bracing it against her chest with a grunt. "Where'd you get this idea of reading to him?"

"His aunt."

"Sara?"

"She said it might cheer him up."

"Cheer him up! Sara? She'd have turned him and Volf both out by now if it wasn't for their pensions. And I don't know as I could blame her. Though he looks after himself as well as you could expect." Mrs Benat hoisted another load onto the table, shook the suds off her swollen hands, and faced her daughter. "Now see here, Alitsia. Sara Chekey's a respectable woman. But you get your ideas from me, not from her. See?"

"Yes, mother."

Lisha was free that afternoon, but did not go to the Chekeys' flat. She took her youngest sister to the park to see the puppet-show, and did not come back till the windy autumn evening was growing dark. That night, in bed, she composed herself in a comfortable but formal position, flat on her back, legs straight, arms along her sides, and set herself to think out what her mother had been saying. It had to do with Sanzo. Did Sara want her and Sanzo to be together? What for? Surely not for the same reason she herself wanted to be with Sanzo. Then what was wrong with it, did her mother think she might fall in love with Sanzo?

There was a slight pause in her mind, and then she thought, But I am. She had not really thought at all, this last week, since the first time he had kissed her; now her mind cleared, everything falling into place as if it had been that way all along. Doesn't she know that? Lisha wondered, since it was now so obvious. Her mother must understand; she always understood things sooner than Lisha did. But she had not been warning Lisha against Sanzo. All she had said was to stay clear of Sara. That was all right. Lisha did not like Sara, and willingly agreed: she wouldn't listen to anything Sara had to say. What had she to say, anyhow? It was nothing to do with her.

"Sanzo," Lisha said with her lips only, not her voice, so that her sister Eva beside her in the bed wouldn't hear; then, content, she turned on her side with her legs curled up and fell asleep.

The next afternoon she went to the Chekeys' flat, and as they sat down as usual at the kitchen table she looked at Sanzo, studying him. His eyes looked all right, only his intent expression gave away his blindness, but one side of his forehead had a crushed look, and you could follow the scarring even under his hair. How queasy did it make her? Did it make her want to get away, as from hydrocephalic children and beggars with two huge nostrils in place of a nose? No; she wanted to touch that scar, very lightly, as he had first touched her face; she wanted to touch his hair, the corners of his mouth, his strong, beautiful, relaxed hands resting on the table as he waited for her to read, or to speak. The only thing that bothered her was a passivity, an unconscious submissiveness, in the way he sat there so quietly waiting. It was not a face or a body made for passivity.

"I don't want to read today," she said.

"All right."

"Do you want to walk? It's lovely out today."

"All right."

He put on his jacket and followed her down the long dark stairs. Out on the street he did not take her arm, though he had not brought his stick; she did not dare take his.

"The park?"

"No. Up the Hill. There's a place I used to go to. Can't make it by myself."

The Hill was the top edge of Rákava; the houses there were old and large, standing in private parks and gardens. Lisha had never walked there before, though it was only about a mile from her own quarter. A broad wind blew from the south along the quiet, unfamiliar streets. She looked about with wonder and pleasure. "They've all got trees on them, all the streets, like a park," she said.

"What are we on, Sovenskar Street?"

"I didn't notice."

"We must be. Is there a grey wall with glass on top across the street, ahead there? We ought to go on up past that."

They reached thus a big unwalled garden, gone wild, at the end of an unpaved drive. Lisha was faintly anxious about trespassing on these silent domains of the wealthy, but Sanzo walked unhesitating, as if he owned them. The drive became steep and the garden widened on up the slope, its lawns and brambles following the contours of the formal park it had once been. At the end of the drive, built almost against the city wall, a square stone house with empty windows stood staring out over the city below.

They sat down on a slope of uncut grass. The low sun was hot, striking through a grove of trees to their left. Smoke or haze overhung the plains beyond the city. All Rákava lay below them. Here and there among the roofs a column of smoke rose till the south wind sheared it off. The dull, heavy sound of the city underlay the stillness of the garden. Sometimes a dog barked far away or they heard for a moment, caught by an echo off the housefronts, the clap of horse-hooves or a calling voice. At the north and east of the city, where the wall was gone, the factories bulked like big blocks set down among toy houses.

"The place still empty?"

Lisha turned to look up at the house with its black, glassless windows. "Looks like it's been empty forever."

"Gardener at one of the other places told me when I was a kid it's been empty for fifty years. Some foreigner built it. Come here and made a fortune with some machinery of his in the mills. Way back. Never sold the place, just left it. It's got forty rooms, he said." Sanzo was lying back in the grass, his arms under his head and his eyes shut; he looked easy, lazy.

"The city's queer from up here. Half all gold and half dark, and all jammed up together, like stuff in a box. I wonder why it's all squeezed together, with all the room around it. The plains go on forever, it looks like."

"I came up here a lot when I was a kid. Liked to look down on it like that. . . . Filthy city."

"It does look beautiful though, from up here."

"Krasnoy, now, there's a beautiful city."

He had lived a year in Krasnoy, in the Veterans' Hospital, after the land mine had blinded him. "You saw it before?" she asked, and he understanding nodded: "In '17, just after I was drafted. I wanted to go back. Krasnoy's big, it's alive, not dead like this place."

"The towers look queer, the Courts and the old prison, all sticking up out of the shadows like somebody's fingers. . . . What did you do when you used to come here?"

"Nothing. Wandered around. Broke into the house a few times."

"Does it really have forty rooms?"

"I never counted. I got spooked in there. You know what's queer? I used to think it was like a blind man. All the black windows."

His voice was quiet, so was his face, kindled with the strong reddish light of the low sun. Lisha watched him awhile, then looked back at the city.

"You can tell that Countess Luisa is going to run out on Liyve," she said, dreamily.

Sanzo laughed, a real laugh of amusement or pleasure, and reached out his hand towards her. When she took it he pulled her back to lie beside him, her head on his shoulder. The weedy turf was as soft as a mattress. Lisha could see nothing over the curve of Sanzo's chest but the sky and the top of the chestnut grove. They lay quiet in the warm dying sunlight, and Lisha was absolutely happy for almost the first time and probably the last time in her life. She was not about to let that go until she had to. It was he who stirred at last and said, "Sun must be down, it's getting cold."

They went back down the wide, calm streets, back into their world. There the streets were noisy and jammed with people coming home from the mills. Sanzo had kept hold of Lisha's hand, so she was able to guide him, but whenever somebody jostled him (no oftener in fact than they jostled her) she felt at fault. Being tall he had to stride, of course, but he did plow straight ahead regardless, and keeping a bit ahead of him to fend off collisions was a job. By the time they got to their building he was frowning as usual, and she was out of breath. They said good night flatly at his entrance, and she stood watching him start up the stairs with that same unhesitating step. Each step taken in darkness.

"Where've you been to?" said a deep voice behind her. She jumped.

"Walking with Sanzo Chekey, father."

Kass Benat, short, broad, and blocky in the twilight, said, "Thought he got about pretty good by himself."

"Yes, he does." Lisha smiled widely. Her father stood before her, solid, pondering. "Go on up," he said finally, and went on to wash himself at the pump in the courtyard.

"She'll get married sometime, you know."

"Maybe," said Mrs Benat.

"What maybe? She's turned eighteen. There's prettier girls but she's a good one. Any day now, she'll marry."

"Not if she's mixed up with that Sanzo she won't."

"Get your pillow over on your side, it's in my eye. What d'you mean, mixed up?"

"How should I know?"

Kass sat up. "What are you telling me?" he demanded hoarsely.

"Nothing. I know that girl. But some of our neighbors could tell you plenty. And each other."

"Why do you let her go there and get talked about, then?"

There was a pause. "Well, because I'm stupid," Mrs Benat said heavily into the darkness. "I just didn't think anything about it. How was I to? He's *blind*."

There was another pause and Kass said, in an uneasy tone, "It isn't Sanzo's fault. He's a good fellow. He was a fine workman. It's not his fault."

"You don't have to tell me. A big good-looking boy like that. And as steady as you were, too. It doesn't make any sense, I'd like to ask the good Lord what he's driving at. . . ."

"Well, all the same. What are you going to do about it?"

"I can handle Sara. She'll give me a handle. I know her. She's got no patience. But that girl . . . If I talk to her again it'll just put more ideas in her head!"

"Talk to him, then."

A longer pause. Kass was half asleep when his wife burst out, "What do you mean, talk to him?"

Kass grunted.

"*You* talk to him, if it's so easy!"

"Turn it off, old lady. I'm tired."

"I wash my hands of it," Mrs Benat said furiously.

Kass reached over and slapped her on the rump. She gave a deep, angry sigh. And they settled down close side by side and slept, while the dark rising wind of autumn scoured the streets and courts.

Old Volf in his windowless bedroom heard the wind prying at the walls, whining. Through the wall Albrekt snored softly, Sara snored deep and slow. After a long time there were creaks and clinks from the kitchen. Volf got up, found his shoes and ragged padded wrapper, and shuffled into the kitchen. No light was on.

"That you, Sanzo?"

"Right."

"Light a candle." He waited, ill at ease in the black darkness. A tin rattled, a match scraped, and around the tiny blue flame the world reappeared.

"Is it lit?"

"Down a little. That's it."

They sat down at the table, Volf trying to pull the wrapper over his legs for warmth. Sanzo was dressed, but his shirt was buttoned wrong; he looked mean and haggard. In front of him on the table were a bottle and a glass. He poured the glass full and pushed it towards his father. Volf got it between his crippled hands and began to drink it in large mouthfuls, with a long savouring pause between each. Tired of waiting, Sanzo got himself another glass, poured it half full, and drank it straight off.

When Volf was done he looked at his son awhile, and said, "Alexander."

"What is it?"

Volf sat looking at him, and finally got up, repeating the name by which no one but Sanzo's mother, fifteen years dead, had ever called him: "Alexander . . ." He touched his son's shoulder with his stiff fingers, stood there a moment, and shuffled back to his room.

Sanzo poured out and drank again. He found it hard to get drunk alone; he wasn't sure if he was drunk yet or not. It was like sitting in a thick fog that never thinned and never got any thicker: a blankness. "Blank, not dark," he said, pointing a finger he could not see at no one there. These words had a great significance, but he did not like the sound of his voice for some reason. He felt for the glass, which had ceased to exist, and drank out of the bottle. The blankness remained the same as before. "Go away, go away, go away," he said. This time he liked the sound of his voice. "You aren't there. None of you. Nobody's there. I'm right here." This was satisfying, but he was beginning to feel sick. "I'm here, God damn it, I'm here," he said loudly. No one answered, no one woke.

No one was there. "I'm here," he said. His mouth was twitching and trembling. He put his head down on his arms to make that stop; he was so dizzy he thought he was falling off the chair, but he fell asleep instead. The candle near his hand burned down and out. He slept on, hunched over the table, while the wind whined and the streets grew dim with morning.

"Well all I said was she was over there a lot lately."

"Yes?" Mrs Benat said in a tone of mild but serious interest.

"And she got all huffy," said Eva, the second daughter, sixteen.

"Mh, she did?"

"He can't even work, what does he act so stuck up for?"

"He works."

"Oh, fixing chairs or something. But he always acts so stuck up, and then she got stuck up when I asked her. Is my hair straight?" Eva was pretty, as her mother had been at sixteen. She was dressed now to walk out with one of the many solemn, bony-wristed youths who requested that privilege, and to earn it had to undergo a close inspection of their persons and their antecedents by Mr and Mrs Benat.

After she had gone Mrs Benat put up her darning and went into the younger children's room. Lisha was humming her five-year-old sister to sleep with the song about the two beggars. The wind that had risen the night before rattled the window in gusts.

"She asleep? Come along."

Lisha followed her mother to the kitchen.

"Make us a cup of chocolate. I'm dead tired. . . . Ough, this little place. If we had a room where you girls could sit with your boys. I don't like this walking out, it's not right. A girl ought to be at home for her courting. . . ."

She said no more until Lisha had made the chocolate and sat down at the table with her. Then she said, "I don't want you going to the Chekeys' any more, Lisha."

Lisha set down her cup. She smoothed out a crease in her skirt, and folded the end of the belt under the buckle.

"Why not, mother?"

"People talk."

"People have to talk about something."

"Not about my daughter."

"Can he come here, then?"

Mrs Benat was startled by this flank attack, bold and almost impudent, the last thing she expected from Lisha. Shaken, she spoke out bluntly: "No. Do you mean you have been courting?"

"I guess so."

"The man is blind, Alitsia!"

"I know," the girl said, without irony.

"He can't—he can't earn a living!"

"His pension's two hundred and fifty."

"Two hundred and fifty!"

"It's two hundred and fifty more than a lot of people are making these days," Lisha said. "Besides, I can work."

"Lisha, you're not talking of marrying him?"

"We haven't yet."

"But Lisha! Don't you see—"

Mrs Benat's voice had grown soft, desperate. She laid the palms of her hands on the table, short, fine hands swollen with hot water and strong soap.

"Lisha, listen to me. I'm forty years old. Half my life I've lived in this city, twenty years in this place, these four rooms. I came here when I was your age. I was born in Foranoy, you know that, it's an old town too, but not a trap like this one. Your grandfather was a mill hand. We had a house there, a house with a parlor, and a yard with a rose bush. When your grandmother was dying, you wouldn't remember, but she kept asking, when are we going home? When are we going home? I liked it fine here at first, I was young, I met your father, we were going to move back up north, in a year or two. And we talked about it. And you children came. And then the war, and good pay. And now that's all gone and it's nothing but strikes and wage cuts. So I finally looked back and saw that we'll never get out, we're here for good. When I saw that I made a vow, Lisha. You'll say I'm not in church from one year to the next, but I went to the cathedral, and I made a vow to the

Virgin of the Sovena there. I said, Holy Mother, I'll stay here, it's all right, if you'll let my children get out. I'll never say another word, if you'll just let them get away, get out of here."

She looked up at her daughter. Her voice grew still softer. "Do you see what I'm getting at, Lisha? Your father's a man in ten thousand. But what has he to show for it? Nothing. Nothing saved. The same flat we moved into when we married. The same job. Practically the same wages. That's how it is in this trap, this city. I see him caught in that, what about you? I won't have it! I want you to marry well, and get out of here! Let me finish. If you married Sanzo Chekey, two can scrape by on that pension of his, but what about children? And there isn't any work for you now. If you married him, you know where you'd go? Across the yard. From four rooms to three. With Sara and Albrekt and the old man. And work for nothing in their ratty little shop. And be tied to a man who'd come to hate you because he couldn't help you. Oh, I know Sanzo, he was always proud, and don't think I haven't grieved for him. But you're my child, and it's your life, Lisha, all your life!"

Her voice had risen, and it quavered on the last words. In tears, Lisha put out her hands across the table and held her mother's tightly. "Listen, mother, I promise . . . if Sanzo ever says anything —maybe he won't, I don't know—if he does, and I still can't find a job, so we'd have enough to move, then I'll say no."

"You don't think he'd let you earn his living?"

Though Lisha's eyes were swollen with tears and her cheeks were wet, she spoke quite steadily. "He's proud," she said, "but he's not stupid, mother."

"But Lisha, can't you find a *whole* man!"

The girl released her hands and sat up straighter. She said nothing.

"Promise me you won't see him again."

"I can't. I promised all I could, mother."

There was a silence between them.

"You never crossed me in anything," Mrs Benat said, in a heavy, pondering tone. "You've been a good one, always. You're grown now. I can't lock you in like a slut. Kass might say yes, but I can't do it now. It's up to you, Lisha. You can save yourself, and him. Or you can waste it all."

"Save myself? For what?" the girl said, without any bitterness. "There never was anybody but him. Even when I was a little kid, before he went into the army. To waste that, that would be a sin. . . . Maybe it was kind of a sin, a little bit, to make that vow, too, mother."

Mrs Benat stood up. "Who's to say?" she asked wearily. "I want to spare my daughter a miserable life, and she tells me it's a sin."

"Not for you, mother. For me. I can't keep your vows!"

"Well, God forgive us both, then. And him. I meant it for the best, Lisha." Mrs Benat went off to her room, walking heavily. Lisha sat on at the table, turning a spoon over and over in her hands. She felt no triumph from having for the first time in her life opposed and defeated her mother. She felt only weariness, and sometimes as she sat tears welled into her eyes again. The only good thing about it all was that there was no longer anyone she feared. At last she went into the room she shared with Eva, found a pencil and a scrap of paper, and wrote a very brief letter to Sanzo Chekey, telling him that she loved him. When it was written she folded it very small, put it in a heavy old gilt-brass locket her mother had given her, and fastened the chain about her neck. Then she went to bed, and lay a long time listening to the endless, aimless blowing of the wind.

Sara Chekey, as Mrs Benat had said, had no patience. That same night she said to her nephew, while Volf and Albrekt were at the tavern, "Sanzo, you ever think about getting married? Don't pull a face like that. I'm serious. I thought of it a while back, I'll tell you why. You should see Lisha Benat's face when she looks at you. That's what put it into my head."

He turned towards Sara and said coolly, "What business of yours is it how she looks at me?"

"I've got eyes, I can see what's in front of me!" Then she caught her breath; but Sanzo gave his disquieting laugh. "Go ahead and look, then," he said. "Only don't bother to tell me."

"Listen, Sanzo Chekey, there you stand in your pride acting like nothing on earth made any difference to you, and never think that what I'm saying might have some sense in it you might listen to. What good do you think I'd get out of your marrying? I was just thinking of you and happened to notice—"

"Drop it," he said. His voice had broken into the strained, arrogant note that exasperated Sara. She turned on him with a rush of justifications and accusations.

"That's done it," Sanzo broke in. "I'll never see that girl again." There being nowhere else to get away from Sara, he went out, slamming the door behind him. He ran down the stairs. Out on the street, without his stick, his coat, or any money, he stopped, and stood there. Lisha wanted to get him, did she? and Sara wanted him got? And they had laid their little plans, and he had fallen for it!—When the awful tension of humiliation and rage began to subside, he had lost his bearings and did not know which direction he was facing, whether he had moved away from the doorway or not. He had to grope around for several minutes to locate himself. People passed by, talking; they paid no attention to him, or thought he was drunk. At last he found the entrance, went back upstairs, took ten kroner from his father's little cashbox, brushed past the protesting Sara, and slammed the door a second time.

He came back about ten the next morning, flopped down on his hallway bed, and slept all day. It was Sunday, and his uncle, having to pass the sprawled figure several times, finally said to Sara, "Why'd he go bust out again? Took all his money, Volf says. He ain't bust out like that all summer. Like he used to when he first got home."

"Yes, drinking up the money that's to support him and his father, that's all he's good for."

Albrekt scratched his head and as usual answered slowly and not exactly to the point. "Seems like a hell of a life for a fellow only twenty-six," he said.

The next day at four Lisha came to the apartment. He proposed that they walk out; they went up onto the Hill, to the garden. It was October now, an overcast day getting ready to rain. Neither of them spoke as they walked. They sat down on the grass below the empty house. Lisha shivered, looking out over the grey city, its thousand streets, its huge factories. Without sunlight, the garden was dominated by the forbidding dark bulk of the chestnut grove. A train whistled across town far away.

"What's it look like?"

"All grey and black."

She heard the childish whispering note in her own voice. But it had not cost his pride to ask the question of her. That was good, that lightened her heart a little. If they could only go on talking, or if he would touch her, so that for him she would be there, then it would be all right. Soon he did reach out to her, and willingly she put herself entirely inside the hold of his arm, resting her cheek against his shoulder. She felt a tension in him as if he had something he wanted to say, and she was about to ask him what it was, when he lifted her face with his hand and kissed her. The kiss grew insistent. He turned so that his weight was on her and pushed her back, the pressure of his mouth sliding down to her throat and to her breasts. She tried to speak and could not, tried to push him away and could not. His weight pushed her down, his shoulder blocked out the sky. Her stomach contracted in a knot, she could not see, but she managed to gasp out, "Let me go," a weak thin whisper. He paid no heed; he crushed her down into the stiff grass and the darkness of the earth, with such strength that she felt only weakness, weakness as if she were dying. But when he tried to force her legs apart with his hand it hurt, so sharply that she began to struggle again, to fight like an animal. She got one arm free, pushed his head away, and writhed out from under him in one convulsive movement. She got to all fours, staggered to her feet, and ran.

Sanzo lay there, his face half buried in the grass.

When she came back to him he had not moved. Her tears, which she had managed to control, started again as she stood by him.

"Come on, get up, Sanzo," she said softly.

He lay still.

"Come on."

After a while he twisted round and sat up. His white face was scored with the crisscross marks of the stiff grass, and his eyes when he opened them looked to the side, as if staring across to the grove of chestnuts.

"Let's go home, Sanzo," she whispered to his terrible face. He drew back his lips and said, "Get away. Let me alone."

"I want to go home."

"Then go! Go on, do you think I need you? Go on, get out!" He tried to push her away, only striking her knee. Lisha went, and waited for him at the side of the drive outside the garden. When he passed her she held her breath, and when he was a good way past her she began to follow him, trying to walk soundlessly. The rain had started, thin drops slanting from a low, quiet sky.

Sanzo did not have his stick. He strode along boldly at first, as he did when he walked with her, but then began to slow down, evidently losing his nerve. He got along all right for a while, and once she heard him whistling his jig-tune through his teeth. Once off the Hill, in the noisier streets where he could not hear echoes, he began to hesitate, lost his bearings and took a wrong turn. Lisha followed close behind him. People stared at both of them. He stopped short at last, and she heard him ask of no one, "Is this Bargay Street?"

A man approaching him stared at him and then answered, "No, you're way off." He took Sanzo's arm and headed him back the right way, with directions, and questions about was he blind, was it a mill accident or the war. Sanzo went off, but before he had gone a block he stopped again and stood there. Lisha caught up with him and took his arm in silence. He was breathing very hard, like an exhausted runner.

"Lisha?"

"Yes. Come on."

But at first he could not move at all, could not take a step.

They went on, slowly, though the rain was getting thicker. When they reached their building he put out his hand to the entranceway, touching the bricks; with that as reassurance he turned to her and said, "Don't come again."

"Good night, Sanzo," she said.

"It's no good, see," he said, and at once started up the stairs. She went on to her entrance.

For several days he went to the furniture store in the afternoon and stayed there late, not coming home till dinner time. Then there was no caning or repairing to be done for a while, and he took to going to the park in the late afternoon. He kept this up after the winter east wind had begun to blow, bringing the rain, the sleet, the thin, damp, dirty snow. When he stayed in the apartment all day, a nervous boredom would grow and grow in him; his hands shook and he lost the sensitivity of his touch, could not tell what he was handling, whether he was handling anything at all. This drove him out, and out longer, until he brought back a headache and a cough. Fever wrung him and rattled him for a week, and left him prey to more coughs and fevers every time he went out.

The weakness, the stupidity of ill health were a relief to him. But it was hard on Sara. She had to leave breakfast ready for him and Volf now, and pay for patent medicines for his headache which sometimes made him cry out in pain, and be waked at night by his coughing. She had never done anything but work hard, and could have compensated herself by nagging and complaining; but it wasn't the work, it was his presence, his always being there, intent, listless, blind, doing nothing, saying nothing. That exasperated her till she would shout at poor Albrekt as they walked to the shop, "I can't stand it, I can't stay in that house with him!"

But the only one who escaped that winter was old Volf. A few nights before Christmas he went out with the ten kroner Sara gave him back monthly from his pension, came back with his bottle, and climbed up three of the four flights of stairs but not the fourth. Heart failure laid him down on the stair-landing, where he was found an hour later. Laid in his coffin he looked a bigger man, and his face in death, intent, unseeing, was a darker version of his son's face. All old friends and neighbors came to the funeral, for which the Chekeys went into debt. The Benats were there, but Sanzo did not hear Lisha's voice.

Sanzo moved out of the hall into the windowless bedroom that had been his father's, and things went on as before, a little easier on Sara.

In January one of Eva's young men, a dyer at the Ferman mill, perhaps discouraged by the competition for Eva, began looking around and saw Lisha. If she saw him it was without fear and without interest; but when he asked her to walk out with him she agreed. She was as quiet and amenable as she had always been, there was no change in her, except that she and her mother were closer friends than they had been, talking together as equals, working together as partners. Her mother certainly saw the young man, but she said nothing about him to Lisha, nor did Lisha say anything except, occasionally, "I'll be walking out with Givan after supper."

Across one night of March the wind from the frozen eastern plains dropped and a humid wind rose up from the south. The rain turned warm and large. In the morning weeds were pushing up between the stones of the courtyard, the city's fountains ran full and noisy, voices carried further down the streets, the sky was dotted with small bluish clouds. That night Lisha and Givan followed one of the Rákava lovers' walks, out through the East Gate to the ruins of a guard tower; and there in the cold and starlight he asked her to marry him. She looked out to the great falling darkness of the Hill and plains, and back to the lights of the city half hidden by the broken outer wall. It took her a long time to answer. "I can't," she said.

"Why not, Lisha?"

She shook her head.

"You were in love with somebody, he went off, or he's already married, or something went wrong with it like that. I know that. I asked you knowing it."

"Why?" she said with anguish. He answered directly: "Because it's over, and it's my time now."

That shook her, and sensing it, he said, with sudden humbleness, "Think about it."

"I will. But—"

"Just think about it. It's the right thing to do, Lisha. I'm the one for you. And I'm not the kind that changes my mind."

That made her smile a little, because of Eva, but also because it was true. He was a shy, determined, hold-fast fellow. What if I did? she thought, and at once felt herself become humble with his humility, protected, certain, safe.

"It's not fair to ask me now," she said with a flash of anger, so that he insisted no more than to ask her, as they parted at her entrance, to think about it. She said she would. And she did.

It was how long, five months now, since the day in the wild garden on the Hill; and she still woke in the night from a dream that the stiff dry grass of autumn was pushing against her back and she could not move or speak or see. Then as she woke from the dream she would see the sky suddenly, and rain falling straight from it on her. It was of that she had to think, only that.

She saw Sanzo oftener now that it was sunny. She always spoke to him. He would be sitting in the yard near the pump sometimes, as his father had used to do. When she came for water for the washing and pressing, she would greet him: "Afternoon, Sanzo."

"That you, Lisha?"

His skin was white and dull, and his hands looked too large on his wrists.

One day in early April she was ironing alone down in the cellar room which her mother rented as a laundry. Light came in through small windows set high in the wall, at ground level; sparse grass and weeds stirred in the sunlight just outside the dusty glass. A streak of sunshine fell across the shirt she was pressing, and the steam rose, smelling sharp of ozone. She began to sing aloud.

> Two tattered beggars met on the street.
> 'Hey, little brother, give me bread to eat!'
> 'Go to the baker's house, ask him for the key,
> If he won't hand it over, say you were sent by me!'

She had to go out for water for the sprinkling-bottle. After the dusk of the cellar, the sunlight filled her eyes with whorls and blots of black and gold. Still humming, she went to the pump. Sanzo had just come out of the house. "Morning, Lisha."

"Morning, Sanzo."

He sat down on the bench, stretching out his long legs, raising his face to the sun. She stood silent by the pump and looked at him. She looked at him intently, judgingly.

"You still there?"

"Yes, I'm here."

"I never see you any more."

She took this in silence. Presently she came and sat down beside him, setting the jug of water down carefully under the bench. "Have you been feeling better?"

"Guess so."

"The sun, it's like we could all get out and live again. It's really spring now. Smell this." She picked the small white flower of a weed that had come up between the flagstones near the pump, and put it in his hand. "It's too little to feel it. Smell it. It smells like pancakes."

He dropped the flower and bowed his head as if looking down at it. "What have you been up to lately? Besides the laundry."

"Oh, I don't know. Eva's getting married, next month. To Ventse Estay. They're going to move to Brailava, up north. He's a bricklayer, there's work up there."

"And how about you?"

"Oh, I'm staying here," she said, and then feeling the dull, cold condescension of his tone added, "I'm engaged."

"Who to?"

"Givan Fenne."

"What's he do?"

"Dyer at Ferman. He's secretary of the Union section."

Sanzo got up, strode across the yard to the archway, then turned and more hesitantly came back. He stood there a couple of yards from her, his hands hanging at his sides; he was not quite facing her. "Good for you, congratulations!" he said, and turned to go.

"Sanzo!"

He stopped and waited.

"Stay here a minute."

"What for?"

"Because I want you to."

He stood still.

"I wanted to tell you . . ." But she got stuck.

He came back, felt for the bench, and sat down. "Look, Lisha," he said in a cooler voice, "it doesn't make any difference."

"Yes it does, it makes a lot. I wanted to tell you that I'm not engaged. He did ask me, but I'm not."

He was listening, but without expression. "Then why'd you say you were?"

"I don't know. To make you mad."

"And so?"

"And so," said Lisha. "And so, I wanted to tell you that you may be blind but that's no excuse for being deaf, dumb, and stupid. I know you were sick and I'm very sorry, but you'd be sicker if I had anything to do with it."

Sanzo sat motionless. "What the hell?" he said. She did not answer; and after quite a while he turned, his hand reaching out and then stopping in mid-gesture, and said nervously, "Lisha?"

"I'm right here."

"Thought you'd gone."

"I'm not done yet."

"Well, go ahead. Nobody's stopping you."

"You are."

A pause.

"Look, Lisha, I have to. Don't you see that?"

"No, I don't. Sanzo, let me explain—"

"No. Don't. I'm not a stone wall, Lisha."

They sat side by side in the warmth a while.

"You'd better marry that fellow."

"I can't."

"Don't be a fool."

"I can't get around it. Around you."

He turned his face away. In a strained, stifled voice he said, "I wanted to apologise—" He made a vague gesture.

"No! Don't."

There was a silence again. Sanzo sat up straighter and rubbed his hands over his eyes and forehead, painfully. "Look, Lisha, it's no good. Honestly. There's your parents, what are they going to say, but that's not it, it's all the rest of it, living with my aunt and uncle, I can't . . . A man has to have something to offer."

"Don't be humble."

"I'm not. I never have been. I know what I am and this—this business doesn't make any difference to that, to me. But it does, it would to somebody else."

"I want to marry you," Lisha said. "If you want to marry me, then do, and if you don't then don't. I can't do it all by myself. But at least remember I'm in on it too!"

"It's you I'm thinking of."

"No it's not. You're thinking of yourself, being blind and the rest of it. You let me think about that, don't think I haven't, either."

"I have thought about you. All winter. All the time. It . . . it doesn't fit, Lisha."

"Not there, no."

"Where, then? Where do we fit? In the house up there on the Hill? We can split it, twenty rooms each. . . ."

"Sanzo, I have to go finish the ironing, it has to be ready at noon. If we decide anything we can figure out that kind of thing. I'd like to get clear out of Rákava."

"Are you," he hesitated. "Will you come this afternoon?"

"All right."

She went off, swinging the water-jug. When she got to the cellar she stood there beside the ironing board and burst into tears. She had not cried for months; she had thought she was too old for tears and would not cry again. She cried without knowing why, her tears ran like a river free of the ice-lock of winter. They ran down her cheeks; she felt neither joy nor grief, and went on with her work long before her tears stopped.

At four o'clock she started to go to the Chekeys' flat, but Sanzo was waiting for her in the courtyard. They went up the Hill to the wild garden, to the lawn above the chestnut grove. The new grass was sparse and soft. In the green darkness of the grove the first candles of the chestnuts burned yellowish-white. A few pigeons soared in the warm, smoky air above the city.

"There's roses all around the house. Would they mind if I picked some?"

"They? Who?"

"All right, I'll be right back."

She came back with a handful of the small, red, thorny roses. Sanzo had lain back with his arms under his head. She sat down by him. The broad, sweet April wind blew over them level with the low sun. "Well," he said, "we haven't got anywhere, have we?"

"I don't know. I think so."

"When did you get like this?"

"Like what?"

"Oh, you know. You used to be different." His voice when he was relaxed had a warm, burring note in it, pleasant to hear. "You never said anything. . . . You know what?"

"What?"

"We never finished reading that book."

He yawned and turned on his side, facing her. She put her hand on his.

"When you were a kid you used to smile all the time. Do you still?"

"Not since I met you," she said, smiling.

Her hand lay still on his.

"Listen. I get the disability pension, two-fifty. It would get us out of Rákava. That's what you want?"

"Yes, I do."

"Well, there's Krasnoy. Unemployment's not supposed to be so bad there, and there must be cheap places to live, it's a bigger city."

"I thought of it too. There must be more jobs there, it's not all one industry like here. I could get something."

"I could pick up something with this caning, if there was anybody with any money wanting things like that done. I can handle repair work too, I was doing some last fall." He seemed to be listening to his own words; and suddenly he gave his strange laugh, that changed his face. "Listen," he said, "this is no good. You going to lead me to Krasnoy by the hand? Forget it. You ought to get away, all right. Clear away. Marry that fellow and get away. Use your head, Lisha."

He had sat up, his arms around his knees, not facing her.

"You talk as if we were both beggars," she said. "As if we had nothing to give each other and nowhere to go."

"That's it. That's the point. We don't. I don't. Do you think getting out of this place will make any difference? Do you think it'll change me? Do you think if I walk around the corner . . . ?" He was trying for irony but achieved only agony. Lisha clenched her hands. "No, of course I don't," she said. "Don't talk like everybody else. They all say that. We can't leave Rákava, we're stuck here. I can't marry Sanzo Chekey, he's blind. We can't do anything we want to do, we haven't got enough money. It's all true, it's all perfectly true. But it's not all. Is it true that if you're a beggar you mustn't beg? What else can you do? If you get a piece of bread do you throw it away? If you felt like I do, Sanzo, you'd take what you were given and hold on to it!"

"Lisha," he said, "oh God, I want to hold on— Nothing—" He reached to her and she came to him; they held each other. He struggled to speak but could not for a long time. "You know I want you, I need you, there is nothing, there is nothing else," he stammered, and she, denying, denying his need, said, "No, no, no, no," but held him with all the strength she had. It was still much less than his. After a while he let her go, and taking her hand stroked it a little. "Look," he said quietly enough, "I do . . . you know. Only it's a very long chance, Lisha."

"We'll never get a chance that isn't long."

"You would."

"You are my long chance," she said, with a kind of bitterness, and a profound certainty.

He found nothing to say to that for a while. Finally he drew a long breath and said very softly, "What you said about begging . . . There was a doctor, two years ago at the hospital where I was, he said something like that, he said what are you afraid of, you see what the dead see, and still you're alive. What have you got to lose?"

"I know what I've got to lose," Lisha said. "And I'm not going to."

"I know what I've got to gain," he said. "That's what scares me." His face was raised, as if he were looking out over the city. It was a very strong face, hard and intent, and Lisha looking at him was shaken; she shut her eyes. She knew that it was she, her will, her presence, that set him free; but she must go with him into freedom, and it was a place she had never been before. In the darkness she whispered, "All right, I'm scared too."

"Well, hang on," he said, putting his arm around her shoulders. "If you hang on, I will."

They sat there, not talking much, as the sun sank into the mist above the plains of April, and the towers and windows of the city yellowed in the falling light. As the sun set they went down the Hill together, out of the silent garden with its beautiful, ruined, staring house, into the smoke and noise and crowding of the thousand streets, where already night had fallen.

1920

The Road East

"THERE IS NO EVIL," Mrs Eray murmured to the rose-geranium in the windowbox, and her son, listening, thought swiftly of caterpillars, cutworms, leafmold, blight; but sunlight shone on the round green leaves and red flowers and grey hair in vast mild assent, and Mrs Eray smiled. Her sleeves dropped back as she raised her arms, a sun-priestess at the window. "Each flower proves it. I'm glad you like flowers, Maler."—"I like trees better," he said, being tired and edgy; edgy was the word he kept thinking, on edge, on the sharp edge. He wanted a vacation badly. "But you couldn't have brought me an oak tree for my birthday!" She laughed, turning to look at the October sheaf of golden asters he had brought her, and he smiled, sunk heavy and passive in his armchair. "Oh you poor old mushroom!" she said, coming to him. A big, pale, heavy man, he disliked that endearment, feeling that it fit him. "Sit up, smile! This lovely day, my birthday, these flowers, the sunlight. How can people refuse to *enjoy* this world! Thank you for my flowers, dear." She kissed his forehead and returned with her buoyant step to the window.

"Ihrenthal's gone," he said.

"Gone?"

"For a week now. No one's even said his name, all week."

It was a frontal attack, for she had known Ihrenthal; he had sat at her dinner-table, a shy, rash, curly-headed man; he had taken a second helping of soup; she could not blow his name away as if it were empty of meaning, of weight.

"You don't know what's become of him?"

"Of course I know."

She traced the round of a geranium leaf with her forefinger and said in a gentle tone as if to the plant, "Not really."

"I don't know whether he's been shot or simply jailed, if that's what you mean."

She withdrew her hand from the plant and stood looking up at the sunlit sky. "You must not be bitter, Maler," she said. "We don't know what's become of him, truly, in the deeper sense. Of him, of all that goes, disappears, is lost to us. We know so little, so very little. And yet enough! The sunlight shines, it bathes us all, it makes no judgment, has no bitterness. That much we know. That's the great lesson. Life is a gift, such a lovely gift! There's no room in it for bitterness. No room." Speaking to the sky, she had not noticed him get up.

"There's room for everything. Too much room. Ihrenthal was my friend. Is his—is his death a lovely gift?" But he rushed and mumbled his words, and she did not have to hear them. He sat down again while she went on to prepare supper and lay the table. "What if I'd been arrested instead of Ihrenthal?" he wanted to say, but did not say. She can't understand, he thought, because she lives inside, she's always looking out the window but she never opens the door, she never goes outside. . . . The tears he could not cry for Ihrenthal strained his throat again, but his thoughts were already slipping away, eastward, towards the road. On the road, the thought of his friend still was with him, the imagination of pain and the knowledge of grief: but with him, not locked inside him. On the road he could walk with sorrow, as he walked through the rain.

The road led east from Krasnoy through farmlands and past

villages to a grey-walled town over which rose the fortress-like tower of an old church. The villages and the town were on maps and he had seen them once from the train: Raskofiu, Ranne, Malenne, Sorg: they were real places, none over fifty miles from the city. But in his mind he walked to them on foot and it was long ago, early in the last century perhaps, for there were no cars on the road nor even railroad crossings. He walked along in rain or sunlight on the country road towards Sorg where at evening he would rest. He would go to an inn down the street from the stout six-sided tower of the church. That was pleasant to look forward to. He had never come to the inn, though once or twice he had entered the town and stood beneath the church portal, a round arch of carven stone. Meantime he walked along through the weather, with a load on his back that varied in weight. On this bright autumn evening he walked too far, till the coming of darkness; it got cold, and fog lay over the dark hollow fields. He had no idea how much farther it was to Sorg, but he was hungry and very tired. He sat down on the bank of the road under a clump of trees and rested there a while in the silence of nightfall. He slipped the packstrap from his shoulders and sat quiet; cold, grieving, and apprehensive, yet quiet, watching mist and dusk. "Supper's ready!" his mother called cheerily. He rose at once and joined her at the table.

Next day he met the gypsy woman. The trolley had brought him east across the river, and he stood waiting to cross its tracks while the wind blew dust down the long street in the long light of evening. Standing beside him she said, "Would you tell me how to get to Geyle Street?" The voice was not a city voice. Black hair, coarse and straight, blew across a colorless face, skin over delicate bone. "I'm going that way," Maler said after a pause, and set off across the street, not looking to see if she came with him. She did. "I never was in Krasnoy before," she said. She came from the plains of a foreign land, windswept plains ringed by far peaks fading into night as nearby, in the wild grass, the smoke of a campfire veered and doubled on the wind over the flames and a woman sang in a strange tongue, a music lost in the huge, blue, frozen dusk. "I've never been out of it, not to speak of," he answered, looking at her. She was about his age, her dress was bright and shoddy, she walked erect, quiet-faced. "What number?" he asked, for they had come to Geyle Street, and she said, "Thirty-three," the number of his house. They walked side by side under the streetlamps, he and this delicate foreign wanderer, strange to each other, walking home together. While getting out his key he explained, "I live in this building," though that really explained very little.

"I'd better ring," she said, "it's a friend of mine that lives here, she's not expecting me," and she looked for the name on the mailboxes. So he could not let her in. But he turned from the open door and asked, "Excuse me, where do you come from?" She looked at him with a slight smile of surprise and answered, "From Sorg."

His mother was in the kitchen. The rose-geranium flared bright in the window, the asters were already fading. On edge, on the edge. He sat in the armchair, his eyes shut, listening for a step overhead or through the wall, the light step that had come to him not across foreign plains with gypsies but down the familiar road in twilight, the road from Sorg leading to this city, this house, this room. Of course the road led westward as well as eastward, only he had never thought of that. He had come in so quietly that his mother had not heard him, and seeing him in the armchair she jumped and her voice rang with panic: "Why didn't you say something, Maler!" Then she lit the lamps and stroked the withering asters and chatted.

The next day he met Provin. He had not yet said a word to Provin, not even good morning, working side by side in the office (Drafting and Planning, Krasnoy Bureau of the State Office of Civil Architecture) on the same plans (State Housing, Trasfiuve Project No. 2). The young man followed him as he left the building at five.

"Mr Eray, let me speak to you."

"What about?"

"About anything," the young man said easily, knowing his own charm, and yet dead serious. He was goodlooking, bearing himself gallantly. Defeated, smoked out of his refuge of silence, Maler said at last, "Well I'm sorry, Provin. Not your fault. Because of Ihrenthal, the man who had your job. Nothing to do with you. It's unreasonable. I'm sorry." He turned away.

Provin said fiercely, "You can't waste hatred like that!"

Maler stood still. "All right. I'll say good morning after this. It's all right. What's the difference? What does it matter to you? What does it matter if any of us talks or doesn't talk? What is there to say?"

"It does matter. There's nothing left to us, now, but one another."

They stood face to face on the street in the fine autumn rain, men passing around them to left and right, and Maler said after a moment, "No, we haven't even got that left, Provin," and set off down Palazay Street to his trolley stop. But after the long ride through midtown and across Old Bridge and through the Trasfiuve, and the walk through rain to Geyle Street, in the doorway of his house he met the woman from Sorg. She asked him, "Can you let me in?"

He nodded, unlocking the door.

"My friend forgot to give me her key, and she had to go out. I've been wandering around, I thought maybe you'd be home around the same time as yesterday. . . ." She was ready to laugh with him at her own improvidence, but he could not laugh or answer her. He had been wrong to reject Provin, dead wrong. He had collaborated with the enemy. Now he must pay the price of his silence, which is more silence, silence when one wants to speak: the gag. He followed her up the stairs, silent. And yet she came from his home, the town where he had never been.

"Good evening," she said at the turning of the stairs, no longer smiling, her quiet face turned away.

"Good evening," he said.

He sat in the armchair and leaned his head back; his mother was in the other room; weariness rose up in him. He was much too tired to travel on the road. Bric-a-brac from the day, the office, the streets milled and juggled in his mind; he was almost asleep. Then for a moment he saw the road, and for the first time he saw people walking on it: other people. Not himself, not Ihrenthal who was dead, not anyone he knew, but strangers, a few people with quiet faces. They were walking westward, towards him, meeting and passing him. He stood still. They looked at him but they did not speak. His mother spoke sharply, "Maler!" He did not move, but she would never pass him by. "Maler, are you ill?" She did not believe in illness, though Maler's father had died of cancer a few years ago; the trouble, she felt, had been in his mind. She had never been sick, and childbirth, even the two miscarriages she had had, had been painless, even joyous. There is no pain, only the fear of it, which one can reject. But she knew that Maler like his father had not rid his mind of fear. "My dear," she murmured, "you mustn't wear yourself out like this."

"I'm all right." All right, all right, everything's all right.

"Is it Ihrenthal?"

She had said the name, she had mentioned the dead, she had admitted death, let it into the room. He stared at her bewildered, overwhelmed with gratitude. She had given him back the power of speech. "Yes," he stammered, "yes, it's that. It's that. I can't take it—"

"You mustn't eat your heart out over it, my dear." She stroked his hand. He sat still, longing for comfort. "It wasn't your fault," she said, the soft exultation coming into her voice again. "There's nothing you could have done to change things, nothing you can do now. He was what he was, perhaps he even sought this, he was rebellious, restless. He's gone his own way. You must stay with what is real, what remains, Maler. His fate led him another way than yours. But yours leads home. When you turn your back on me, when you won't speak to me, my dear, then you're rejecting not only me, but your true self. After all, we have no one but each other."

He said nothing, bitterly disappointed, borne down by his guilt towards her, who did depend wholly on him, and towards Ihrenthal and Provin from whom he had tried to escape, following an unreal road in silence and alone. But when she raised her arms and said or sang, "Nothing is evil, nothing is wasted, if only we look at the world without fear!"—then he broke away and stood up. "The only way to do that is go blind," he said, and went out, letting the door slam.

He came back drunk at three in the morning, singing. He woke too late to shave, and was late to work; after the lunch hour he did not go back to the office. He sat on in the dark simmering bar behind Roukh Palace where he and Ihrenthal had used to lunch together on beer and herring, and by six, when Provin came in, he was drunk again. "Good evening, Provin! Have a drink on me."

"Thanks, I will. Givaney said you might be here." They drank in silence, side by side, jammed together by the press at the bar. Maler straightened up and said, "There is no evil, Provin."

"No?" said Provin, smiling, glancing up at him.

"No. None at all. People get in trouble for things they say, but when they're shot for it it's their own fault, eh, so there's nothing evil in that. Or if they're just put in jail, all the better, it keeps them from talking. If nobody talks then nobody tells lies, and there isn't any real evil, you see, only lies. Evil is a lie. You have to be silent, then the world's good. All good. The police are good men with wives and families, the agents are good patriotic men, the soldiers are good, the State is good, we're good citizens of a great country, only we mustn't speak. We mustn't talk to one another, in case we tell a lie. That would spoil it all. Never speak to a man. Especially never speak to a woman. Have you got a mother, Provin? I don't. I was born of a virgin, painlessly. Pain is a lie, it doesn't exist— see?" He brought his hand down backwards on the edge of the bar with a crack like a stick breaking. "Ah!" he cried, and Provin too turned white. The men at the bar all round them, dark-faced men in shoddy grey, glanced at him; the simmering murmur of their talk went on. The month on the calendar over the bar was October, 1956. Maler pressed his hand to his side under his coat for a while and then silently, left-handed, finished his beer. "In Budapest, on Wednesday," the man next to him repeated quietly to his neighbor in plasterer's overalls, "on Wednesday."

"Is that true, all that?"

Provin nodded. "It's true."

"Are you from Sorg, Provin?"

"No, from Raskofiu, a few miles this side of Sorg. Will you come home with me, Mr Eray?"

"Too drunk."

"My wife and I have a room to ourselves. I wanted to talk with you. This business." He nodded at the man in overalls. "There's a chance—"

"Too late," Maler said. "Too drunk. Listen, do you know the road between Raskofiu and Sorg?"

Provin looked down. "You come from there too?"

"No. I was born here in Krasnoy. City boy. Never been to Sorg. Saw the church-spire once from a train going east, doing my military service. Now I think I'll go see it closer up. When will the trouble start here?" he asked conversationally as they left the bar, but the young man did not answer. Maler walked back across the river to Geyle Street, a very long walk. He was sober when he got home. His mother looked hard and shrunken, like a nut dried around its kernel. He was her lie, and one must keep hold of a lie, wither around it, hold on. Her world without evil, without hope, her world without revolution depended on him alone.

While he ate his late dry supper she asked him about the rumors she had heard at market. "Yes," he said, "that's right. And the West is going to help them, send in airplanes with guns, troops maybe. They'll make it." Then he laughed, and she dared not ask him why. Next day he went to work as usual. But on Saturday morning early the woman from Sorg stood at his door. "Please, can you get me across the river?" Softly, not to wake his mother, he asked what she meant. She explained that the bridges were being guarded and they would not let her across since she had no Krasnoy domicile card, and she must get across to the railway station to go back to her family in Sorg. She was a day late already, she must get back. "If you're going to work and I went with you, you see, they might let you cross. . . ."

"My office won't be open," he said.

She said nothing.

"I don't know, we could try it," he said, looking down at her, feeling himself stout and heavy in his dressing-gown. "Are the trolleys running?"

"No, they've stopped, people say everything's stopped. Maybe even the trains. It's going on over there on the west side, in River Quarter, they say."

In the early light under a grey sky they went together through the long streets toward the river. "They'll probably stop me," he said, "I'm only an architect. If they do, you might try to get to Grasse somehow. The trains going east stop there, it's a suburban station. It's only five or six miles from Krasnoy." She nodded. She wore the same bright shoddy dress; it was cold, and they walked fast. When they came in sight of Old Bridge they hesitated. Across the bridge between the fine stone balustrades stood not only the idling soldiers they had expected but also a huge black thing, hunchbacked and oblique, its machine-gun snout poked out towards the west. A soldier waved aside his identification cards, told him to go home. He and the woman returned up the long streets where no trolleys ran, no cars, and few people walked. "If you want to walk on out to Grasse," he said, "I'll go with you."

The coarse black hair whipped over her cheek as she smiled, bewildered, a countrywoman astray. "You're kind. But will the trains be running?"

"Probably not."

The colorless delicate face was bent pondering; she smiled a little, faced with the insuperable.

"Have you children at home, in Sorg?"

"Yes, two children. I was here trying to get my husband's compensation, he was hurt in an accident at the mill, he lost his arm. . . ."

"It's about forty miles to Sorg. Walking, you might be there tomorrow night."

"I was thinking that. But with this trouble they'll be policing the ways out of the city, all the roads. . . ."

"Not the roads east."

"I'm a bit scared," she said after a while, gently; no gypsy from the wild lands but only a countrywoman on the roads of ruin, afraid to go alone. She need not go alone. They could walk together out of the city eastward, taking the road up to Grasse and then down among the hills, from town to town on the rolling plain past fields and lone farms until they came in autumn evening under the grey walls, to the high spire of Sorg; and now with the trouble in Krasnoy the roads would be quite empty, no buses, no cars running, as if they walked into the last century and on before into the other centuries, back, towards their heritage, away from their death.

"You'd best wait it out here," he said as they turned onto Geyle Street. She looked up at his heavy face, saying nothing. On the stair-landing she murmured, "Thank you. You were kind to go with me."

"I wish I could." He turned to his door.

In the afternoon the windows of the flat rattled and rattled. His mother sat with her hands in her lap staring out over the flowers of the geranium at the cloud-spotted sky full of sunshine. "I'm going out, mother," Maler said, and she sat still; but as he put on his coat she said, "It's not safe."

"No. It's not safe."

"Stay inside, Maler."

"It's sunny outside. The sunshine bathes us all, eh? I need a good bath."

She looked up at him in terror. Having denied the need for help, she did not know how to ask for it. "This isn't real, this is insane, all this trouble-making, you mustn't get mixed up in it, I won't accept it. I won't believe it!" she said, raising her long arms to him as if in incantation. He stood there, a big heavy man. Down on the street there was a long shout, silence, a shout; the windows rattled again. She dropped her arms to her sides and cried, "But Maler, I'll be alone!"

"Yes, well," he said softly, thoughtfully, not wanting to hurt her, "that's how it is." He left her, closed the door behind him, and went down the stairs and out, dazzled at first by the bright October sunlight, to join the army of the unarmed and with them to go down the long streets leading westward to, but not across, the river.

1956

Brothers and Sisters

THE INJURED QUARRIER lay on a high hospital bed. He had not recovered consciousness. His silence was grand and oppressive; his body under the sheet that dropped in stiff folds, his face were as indifferent as stone. The mother, as if challenged by that silence and indifference, spoke loudly: "What did you do it for? Do you want to die before I do? Look at him, look at him, my beauty, my hawk, my river, my son!" Her sorrow boasted of itself. She rose to the occasion like a lark to the morning. His silence and her outcry meant the same thing: the unendurable made welcome. The younger son stood listening. They bore him down with their grief as large as life. Unconscious, heedless, broken like a piece of chalk, that body, his brother, bore him down with the weight of the flesh, and he wanted to run away, to save himself.

The man who had been saved stood beside him, a little stooped fellow, middle-aged, limestone dust white in his knuckles. He too was borne down. "He saved my life," he said to Stefan, gaping, wanting an explanation. His voice was the flat toneless voice of the deaf.

"He would," Stefan said. "That's what he'd do."

He left the hospital to get his lunch. Everybody asked him about his brother. "He'll live," Stefan said. He went to the White Lion for lunch, drank too much. "Crippled? Him? Kostant? So he got a couple of tons of rock in the face, it won't hurt him, he's made of the stuff. He wasn't born, he was quarried out." They laughed at him as usual. "Quarried out," he said. "Like all the rest of you." He left the White Lion, went down Ardure Street four blocks straight out of town, and kept on straight, walking northeast, parallel with the railroad tracks a quarter mile away. The May sun was small and greyish overhead. Underfoot there were dust and small weeds. The Karst, the limestone plain, jigged tinily about him with heatwaves like the transparent vibrating wings of flies. Remote and small, rigid beyond that vibrant greyish haze, the mountains stood. He had known the mountains from far off all his life, and twice had seen them close, when he took the Brailava train, once going, once coming back. He knew they were clothed in trees, fir trees with roots clutching the banks of running streams and with branches dark in the mist that closed and parted in the mountain gullies in the light of dawn as the train clanked by, its smoke dropping down the green slopes like a dropping veil. In the mountains the streams ran noisy in the sunlight; there were waterfalls. Here on the karst the rivers ran underground, silent in dark veins of stone. You could ride a horse all day from Sfaroy Kampe and still not reach the mountains, still be in the limestone dust; but late on the second day you would come under the shade of trees, by running streams. Stefan Fabbre sat down by the side of the straight unreal road he had been walking on, and put his head in his arms. Alone, a mile from town, a quarter mile from the tracks, sixty miles from the mountains, he sat and cried for his brother. The plain of dust and stone quivered and grimaced about him in the heat like the face of a man in pain.

He got back an hour late from lunch to the office of the Chorin Company where he worked as an accountant. His boss came to his desk: "Fabbre, you needn't stay this afternoon."

"Why not?"

"Well, if you want to go to the hospital . . ."

"What can I do there? I can't sew him back up, can I?"

"As you like," the boss said, turning away.

"Not me that got a ton of rocks in the face, is it?" Nobody answered him.

When Kostant Fabbre was hurt in the rockslide in the quarry he was twenty-six years old; his brother was twenty-three; their sister Rosana was thirteen. She was beginning to grow tall and sullen, to weigh upon the earth. Instead of running, now, she walked, ungainly and somewhat hunched, as if at each step she crossed, unwilling, a threshold. She talked loudly, and laughed aloud. She struck back at whatever touched her, a voice, a wind, a word she did not understand, the evening star. She had not learned indifference, she knew only defiance. Usually she and Stefan quarrelled, touching each other where each was raw, unfinished. This night when he got home the mother had not come back from the hospital, and Rosana was silent in the silent house. She had been thinking all afternoon about pain, about pain and death; defiance had failed her.

"Don't look so down," Stefan told her as she served out beans for supper. "He'll be all right."

"Do you think . . . Somebody was saying he might be, you know. . . ."

"Crippled? No, he'll be all right."

"Why do you think he, you know, ran to push that fellow out of the way?"

"No why to it, Ros. He just did it."

He was touched that she asked these questions of him, and surprised at the certainty of his answers. He had not thought that he had any answers.

"It's queer," she said.

"What is?"

"I don't know. Kostant . . ."

"Knocked the keystone out of your arch, didn't it? Wham! One rock falls, they all go." She did not understand him; she did not recognise the place where she had come today, a place where she was like other people, sharing with them the singular catastrophe of being alive. Stefan was not the one to guide her. "Here we all are," he went on, "lying around each of us under our private pile of rocks. At least they got Kostant out from under his and filled him up with morphine. . . . D'you remember once when you were little you said 'I'm going to marry Kostant when I grow up.' "

Rosana nodded. "Sure. And he got real mad."

"Because mother laughed."

"It was you and dad that laughed."

Neither of them was eating. The room was close and dark around the kerosene lamp.

"What was it like when dad died?"

"You were there," Stefan said.

"I was nine. But I can't remember it. Except it was hot like now, and there were a lot of big moths knocking their heads on the glass. Was that the night he died?"

"I guess so."

"What was it like?" She was trying to explore the new land.

"I don't know. He just died. It isn't like anything else."

The father had died of pneumonia at forty-six, after thirty years in the quarries. Stefan did not remember his death much more clearly than Rosana did. He had not been the keystone of the arch.

"Have we got any fruit to eat?"

The girl did not answer. She was gazing at the air above the place at the table where the elder brother usually sat. Her forehead and dark eyebrows were like his, were his: likeness between kin is identity, the brother and sister were, by so much or so little, the curve of brow and temple, the same person; so that, for a moment, Kostant sat across the table mutely contemplating his own absence.

"Is there any?"

"I think there's some apples in the pantry," she answered, coming back to herself, but so quietly that in her brother's eyes she seemed briefly a woman, a quiet woman speaking out of her thoughts; and he said with tenderness to that woman, "Come on, let's go over to the hospital. They must be through messing with him by now."

The deaf man had come back to the hospital. His daughter was with him. Stefan knew she clerked at the butcher's shop. The deaf man, not allowed into the ward, kept Stefan half an hour in the hot, pine-floored waiting room that smelled of disinfectant and resin. He talked, walking about, sitting down, jumping up, arguing in the loud even monotone of his deafness. "I'm not going back to the pit. No sir. What if I'd said last night I'm not going into the pit tomorrow? Then how'd it be now, see? I wouldn't be here now, nor you wouldn't, nor he wouldn't, him in there, your brother. We'd all be home. Home safe and sound, see? I'm not going back to the pit. No, by God. I'm going out to the farm, that's where I'm going. I grew up there, see, out west in the foothills there, my brother's there. I'm going back and work the farm with him. I'm not going back to the pit again."

The daughter sat on the wooden bench, erect and still. Her face was narrow, her black hair was pulled back in a knot. "Aren't you hot?" Stefan asked her, and she answered gravely, "No, I'm all right." Her voice was clear. She was used to speaking to her deaf father. When Stefan said nothing more she looked down again and sat with her hands in her lap. The father was still talking. Stefan rubbed his hands through his sweaty hair and tried to interrupt. "Good, sounds like a good plan, Sachik. Why waste the rest of your life in the pits." The deaf man talked right on.

"He doesn't hear you."

"Can't you take him home?"

"I couldn't make him leave here even for dinner. He won't stop talking."

Her voice was much lower saying this, perhaps from embarrassment, and the sound of it caught at Stefan. He rubbed his sweaty hair again and stared at her, thinking for some reason of smoke, waterfalls, the mountains.

"You go on home." He heard in his own voice the qualities of hers, softness and clarity. "I'll get him over to the Lion for an hour."

"Then you won't see your brother."

"He won't run away. Go on home."

At the White Lion both men drank heavily. Sachik talked on about the farm in the foothills, Stefan talked about the mountains and his year at college in the city. Neither heard the other. Drunk, Stefan walked Sachik home to one of the rows of party-walled houses that the Chorin Company had put up in '95 when they opened the new quarry. The houses were on the west edge of town, and behind them the karst stretched in the light of the half-moon away on and on, pocked, pitted, level, answering the moonlight with its own pallor taken at third-hand from the sun. The moon, second-hand, worn at the edges, was hung up in the sky like something a housewife leaves out to remind her it needs mending. "Tell your daughter everything is all right," Stefan said, swaying at the door. "Everything is all right," Sachik repeated with enthusiasm, "aa-all right."

Stefan went home drunk, and so the day of the accident blurred in his memory into the rest of the days of the year, and the fragments that stayed with him, his brother's closed eyes, the dark girl looking at him, the moon looking at nothing, did not recur to his mind together as parts of a whole, but separately with long intervals between.

On the karst there are no springs; the water they drink in Sfaroy Kampe comes from deep wells and is pure, without taste. Ekata Sachik tasted the strange spring-water of the farm still on her lips as she scrubbed an iron skillet at the sink. She scrubbed with a stiff brush, using more energy than was needed, absorbed in the work deep below the level of conscious pleasure. Food had been burned in the skillet, the water she poured in fled brown from the bristles of the brush, glittering in the lamplight. They none of them knew how to cook here at the farm. Sooner or later she would take over the cooking and they could eat properly. She liked housework, she liked to clean, to bend hot-faced to the oven of a woodburning range, to call people in to supper; lively, complex work, not a bore like clerking at the butcher's shop, making change, saying "Good day" and "Good day" all day. She had left town with her family because she was sick of that. The farm family had taken the four of them in without comment, as a natural disaster, more mouths to feed, but also more hands to work. It was a big, poor farm.

Ekata's mother, who was ailing, crept about behind the bustling aunt and cousin; the men, Ekata's uncle, father, and brother, tromped in and out in dusty boots; there were long discussions about buying another pig. "It's better here than in the town, there's nothing in the town," Ekata's widowed cousin said; Ekata did not answer her. She had no answer. "I think Martin will be going back," she said finally, "he never thought to be a farmer." And in fact her brother, who was sixteen, went back to Sfaroy Kampe in August to work in the quarries.

He took a room in a boarding house. His window looked down on the Fabbres' back yard, a fenced square of dust and weeds with a sad-looking fir tree at one corner. The landlady, a quarrier's widow, was dark, straight-backed, calm, like Martin's sister Ekata. With her the boy felt manly and easy. When she was out, her daughter and the other boarders, four single men in their twenties, took over; they laughed and slapped one another on the back; the railway clerk from Brailava would take out his guitar and play music-hall songs, rolling his eyes like raisins set in lard. The daughter, thirty and unmarried, would laugh and move about a great deal, her shirtwaist would come out of her belt in back and she would not tuck it in. Why did they make so much fuss? Why did they laugh, punch one another's shoulders, play the guitar and sing? They would begin to make fun of Martin. He would shrug and reply gruffly. Once he replied in the language used in the quarry pits. The guitar player took him aside and spoke to him seriously about how one must behave in front of ladies. Martin listened with his red face bowed. He was a big, broad-shouldered boy. He thought he might pick up this clerk from Brailava and break his neck. He did not do it. He had no right to. The clerk and the others were men; there was something they understood which he did not understand, the reason why they made a fuss, rolled their eyes, played and sang. Until he understood that, they were justified in telling him how to speak to ladies. He went up to his room and leaned out the window to smoke a cigarette. The smoke hung in the motionless evening air which enclosed the fir tree, the roofs, the world in a large dome of hard, dark-blue crystal. Rosana

Fabbre came out into the fenced yard next door, dumped out a pan of dishwater with a short, fine swing of her arms, then stood still to look up at the sky, foreshortened, a dark head over a white blouse, caught in the blue crystal. Nothing moved for sixty miles in all directions except the last drops of water in the dishpan, which one by one fell to the ground, and the smoke of Martin's cigarette curling and dropping away from his fingers. Slowly he drew in his hand so that her eye would not be caught by the tiny curl of smoke. She sighed, whacked the dishpan on the jamb of the door to shake out the last drops, which had already run out, turned, went in; the door slammed. The blue air rejoined without a flaw where she had stood. Martin murmured to that flawless air the word he had been advised not to say in front of ladies, and in a moment, as if in answer, the evening star shone out northwestwards high and clear.

Kostant Fabbre was home, and alone all day now that he was able to get across a room on crutches. How he spent these vast silent days no one considered, probably least of all himself. An active man, the strongest and most intelligent worker in the quarries, a crew foreman since he was twenty-three, he had had no practice at all at idleness, or solitude. He had always used his time to the full in work. Now time must use him. He watched it at work upon him without dismay or impatience, carefully, like an apprentice watching a master. He employed all his strength to learn his new trade, that of weakness. The silence in which he passed the days clung to him now as the limestone dust had used to cling to his skin.

The mother worked in the dry-goods shop till six; Stefan got off work at five. There was an hour in the evening when the brothers were together alone. Stefan had used to spend this hour out in the back yard under the fir tree, stupid, sighing, watching swallows dart after invisible insects in the interminably darkening air, or else he had gone to the White Lion. Now he came home promptly, bringing Kostant the *Brailava Messenger*. They both read it, exchanging sheets. Stefan planned to speak, but did not. The dust lay on his lips. Nothing happened. Over and over the same hour passed. The older brother sat still, his handsome, quiet face bowed over the newspaper. He read slowly; Stefan had to wait to exchange sheets; he could see Kostant's eyes move from word to word. Then Rosana would come in yelling good-bye to schoolmates in the street, the mother would come in, doors would bang, voices ring from room to room, the kitchen would smoke and clatter, plates clash, the hour was gone.

One evening Kostant, having barely begun to read, laid the newspaper down. There was a long pause which contained no events and which Stefan, reading, pretended not to notice.

"Stefan, my pipe's there by you."

"Oh, sure," Stefan mumbled, took him his pipe. Kostant filled and lit it, drew on it a few times, set it down. His right hand lay on the arm of the chair, hard and relaxed, holding in it a knot of desolation too heavy to lift. Stefan hid behind his paper and the silence went on.

I'll read out this about the union coalition to him, Stefan thought, but he did not. His eyes insisted on finding another article, reading it. Why can't I talk to him?

"Ros is growing up," Kostant said.

"She's getting on," Stefan mumbled.

"She'll take some looking after. I've been thinking. This is no town for a girl growing up. Wild lads and hard men."

"You'll find them anywhere."

"Will you; no doubt," Kostant said, accepting Stefan's statement without question. Kostant had never been off the karst, never been out of Sfaroy Kampe. He knew nothing at all but limestone, Ardure Street and Chorin Street and Gulhelm Street, the mountains far off and the enormous sky.

"See," he said, picking up his pipe again, "she's a bit wilful, I think."

"Lads will think twice before they mess with Fabbre's sister," Stefan said. "Anyhow, she'll listen to you."

"And you."

"Me? What should she listen to me for?"

"For the same reasons," Kostant said, but Stefan had found his voice now—"What should she respect me for? She's got good enough sense. You and I didn't listen to anything dad said, did we? Same thing."

"You're not like him. If that's what you meant. You've had an education."

"An education, I'm a real professor, sure. Christ! One year at the Normal School!"

"Why did you fail there, Stefan?"

The question was not asked lightly; it came from the heart of Kostant's silence, from his austere, pondering ignorance. Unnerved at finding himself, like Rosana, included so deeply in the thoughts of this reserved and superb brother, Stefan said the first thing that came to mind—"I was afraid I'd fail. So I didn't work."

And there it was, plain as a glass of water, the truth, which he had never admitted to himself.

Kostant nodded, thinking over this idea of failure, which was surely not one familiar to him; then he said in his resonant, gentle voice, "You're wasting your time here in Kampe."

"I am? What about yourself?"

"I'm wasting nothing. I never won any scholarship." Kostant smiled, and the humor of his smile angered Stefan.

"No, you never tried, you went straight to the pit at fifteen. Listen, did you ever wonder, did you ever stop a minute to ask what am I doing here, why did I go into the quarries, what do I work there for, am I going to work there six days a week every week of the year every year of my life? For pay, sure, there's other ways to make a living. What's it *for?* Why does anybody stay here, in this Godforsaken town on this Godforsaken piece of rock where nothing grows? Why don't they get up and go somewhere? Talk about wasting your time! What in God's name is it all for—is this all there is to it?"

"I have thought that."

"I haven't thought anything else for years."

"Why not go, then?"

"Because I'm afraid to. It'd be like Brailava, like the college. But you—"

"I've got my work here. It's mine, I can do it. Anywhere you go, you can still ask what it's all for."

"I know." Stefan got up, a slight man moving and talking restlessly, half finishing his gestures and words. "I know. You take yourself with yourself. But that means one thing for me and something else again for you. You're wasting yourself here, Kostant. It's the same as this business, this hero business, smashing yourself up for that Sachik, a fool who can't even see a rockslide coming at him—"

"He couldn't *hear* it," Kostant put in, but Stefan could not stop now. "That's not the point; the point is, let that kind of man look after himself, what's he to you, what's his life to you? Why did you go in after him when you saw the slide coming? For the same reason as you went into the pit, for the same reason as you keep working in the pit. For no reason. Because it just came up. It just happened. You let things happen to you, you take what's handed you, when you could take it all in your hands and do what you wanted with it!"

It was not what he had meant to say, not what he had wanted to say. He had wanted Kostant to talk. But words fell out of his own mouth and bounced around him like hailstones. Kostant sat quiet, his strong hand closed not to open; finally he answered: "You're making something of me I'm not." That was not humility. There was none in him. His patience was that of pride. He understood Stefan's yearning but could not share it, for he lacked nothing; he was intact. He would go forward in the same, splendid, vulnerable integrity of body and mind towards whatever came to meet him on his road, like a king in exile on a land of stone, bearing all his kingdom—cities, trees, people, mountains, fields and flights of birds in spring—in his closed hand, a seed for the sowing; and, because there was no one of his language to speak to, silent.

"But listen, you said you've thought the same thing, what's it all for, is this all there is to life—If you've thought that, you must have looked for the answer!"

After a long pause Kostant said, "I nearly found it. Last May."

Stefan stopped fidgeting, looked out the front window in silence. He was frightened. "That—that's not an answer," he mumbled.

"Seems like there ought to be a better one," Kostant agreed.

"You get morbid sitting here. . . . What you need's a woman," Stefan said, fidgeting, slurring his words, staring out at the early-autumn evening rising from stone pavements unobscured by tree-branches or smoke, even, clear, and empty. Behind him, his brother laughed. "It's the truth," Stefan said bitterly, not turning.

"Could be. How about yourself?"

"They're sitting out on the steps there at widow Katalny's. She must be night nursing at the hospital again. Hear the guitar? That's the fellow from Brailava, works at the railway office, goes after anything in skirts. Even goes after Nona Katalny. Sachik's kid lives there now. Works in the New Pit, somebody said. Maybe in your crew."

"What kid?"

"Sachik's."

"Thought he'd left town."

"He did, went to some farm in the west hills. This is his kid, must have stayed behind to work."

"Where's the girl?"

"Went with her father as far as I know."

The pause this time lengthened out, stretched around them like a pool in which their last words floated, desultory, vague, fading. The room was full of dusk. Kostant stretched and sighed. Stefan felt peace come into him, as intangible and real as the coming of the darkness. They had talked, and got nowhere; it was not a last step; the next step would come in its time. But for a moment he was at peace with his brother, and with himself.

"Evenings getting shorter," Kostant said softly.

"I've seen her once or twice. Saturdays. Comes in with a farm wagon."

"Where's the farm at?"

"West, in the hills, was all old Sachik said."

"Might ride out there, if I could," Kostant said. He struck a match for his pipe. The flare of the match in the clear dusk of the room was also a peaceful thing; when Stefan looked back at the window the evening seemed darker. The guitar had stopped and they were laughing out on the steps next door.

"If I see her Saturday I'll ask her to come by."

Kostant said nothing. Stefan wanted no answer. It was the first time in his life that his brother had asked his help.

The mother came in, tall, loud-voiced, tired. Floors cracked and cried under her step, the kitchen clashed and steamed, everything was noisy in her presence except her two sons, Stefan who eluded her, Kostant who was her master.

Stefan got off work Saturdays at noon. He sauntered down Ardure Street looking out for the farm wagon and roan horse. They were not in town, and he went to the White Lion, relieved and bored. Another Saturday came and a third. It was October, the afternoons were shorter. Martin Sachik was walking down Gulhelm Street ahead of him; he caught up and said, "Evening, Sachik." The boy looked at him with blank grey eyes; his face, hands, and clothes were grey with stone-dust and he walked as slowly and steadily as a man of fifty.

"Which crew are you in?"

"Five." He spoke distinctly, like his sister.

"That's my brother's."

"I know." They went on pace for pace. "They said he might be back in the pit next month."

Stefan shook his head.

"Your family still out there on that farm?" he asked.

Martin nodded, as they stopped in front of the Katalny house. He revived, now that he was home and very near dinner. He was flattered by Stefan Fabbre's speaking to him, but not shy of him. Stefan was clever, but he was spoken of as a moody, unsteady fellow, half a man where his brother was a man and a half. "Near Verre," Martin said. "A hell of a place. I couldn't take it."

"Can your sister?"

"Figures she has to stay with Ma. She ought to come back. It's a hell of a place."

"This isn't heaven," Stefan said.

"Work your head off there and never get any money for it, they're all loony on those farms. Right where Dad belongs." Martin felt virile, speaking disrespectfully of his father. Stefan Fabbre looked at him, not with respect, and said, "Maybe. Evening to you, Sachik." Martin went into the house defeated. When was he going to become a man, not subject to other men's reproof? Why did it matter if Stefan Fabbre looked at him and turned away? The next day he met Rosana Fabbre on the street. She was with a girl friend, he with a fellow quarrier; they had all been in school together last year. "How you doing, Ros?" Martin said loudly, nudging his friend. The girls walked by haughty as cranes. "There's a hot one," Martin said. "Her? She's just a kid," the friend said. "You'd be surprised," Martin told him with a thick laugh, then looked up and saw Stefan Fabbre crossing the street. For a moment he realised that he was surrounded, there was no escape.

Stefan was on the way to the White Lion, but passing the town hotel and livery stable he saw the roan horse in the yard. He went in, and sat in the brown parlour of the hotel in the smell of harness grease and dried spiders. He sat there two hours. She came in, erect, a black kerchief on her hair, so long awaited and so fully herself that he watched her go by with simple pleasure, and only woke as she started up the stairs. "Miss Sachik," he said.

She stopped, startled, on the stairs.

"Wanted to ask you a favor." Stefan's voice was thick after the strange timeless waiting. "You're staying here over tonight?"

"Yes."

"Kostant was asking about you. Wanted to ask about your father. He's still stuck indoors, can't walk much."

"Father's fine."

"Well, I wondered if—"

"I could look in. I was going to see Martin. It's next door, isn't it?"

"Oh, fine. That's—I'll wait."

Ekata ran up to her room, washed her dusty face and hands, and put on, to decorate her grey dress, a lace collar that she had brought to wear to church tomorrow. Then she took it off again.

She retied the black kerchief over her black hair, went down, and walked with Stefan six blocks through the pale October sunlight to his house. When she saw Kostant Fabbre she was staggered. She had never seen him close to except in the hospital where he had been effaced by casts, bandages, heat, pain, her father's chatter. She saw him now.

They fell to talking quite easily. She would have felt wholly at ease with him if it had not been for his extraordinary beauty, which distracted her. His voice and what he said was grave, plain, and reassuring. It was the other way round with the younger brother, who was nothing at all to look at, but with whom she felt ill at ease, at a loss. Kostant was quiet and quieting; Stefan blew in gusts like autumn wind, bitter and fitful; you didn't know where you were with him.

"How is it for you out there?" Kostant was asking, and she replied, "All right. A bit dreary."

"Farming's the hardest work, they say."

"I don't mind the hard, it's the muck I mind."

"Is there a village near?"

"Well, it's halfway between Verre and Lotima. But there's neighbors, everybody within twenty miles knows each other."

"We're still your neighbors, by that reckoning," Stefan put in. His voice slurred off in mid-sentence. He felt irrelevant to these two. Kostant sat relaxed, his lame leg stretched out, his hands clasped round the other knee; Ekata faced him, upright, her hands lying easy in her lap. They did not look alike but might have been brother and sister. Stefan got up with a mumbled excuse and went out back. The north wind blew. Sparrows hopped in the sour dirt under the fir tree and the scurf of weedy grass. Shirts, underclothes, a pair of sheets snapped, relaxed, jounced on the clothesline between two iron posts. The air smelt of ozone. Stefan vaulted the fence, cut across the Katalny yard to the street, and walked westward. After a couple of blocks the street petered out. A track led on to a quarry, abandoned twenty years ago when they struck water; there was twenty feet of water in it now. Boys swam there, summers. Stefan had swum there, in terror, for he had never learned to swim well and there was no foothold, it was all deep and bitter cold. A boy had drowned there years ago, last year a man had drowned himself, a quarrier going blind from stone-splinters in his eyes. It was still called the West Pit. Stefan's father had worked in it as a boy. Stefan sat down by the lip of it and watched the wind, caught down in the four walls, eddy in tremors over the water that reflected nothing.

"I have to go meet Martin," Ekata said. As she stood up Kostant put a hand out to his crutches, then gave it up: "Takes me too long to get afoot," he said.

"How much can you get about on those?"

"From here to there," he said, pointing to the kitchen. "Leg's all right. It's the back's slow."

"You'll be off them—?"

"Doctor says by Easter. I'll run out and throw 'em in the West Pit. . . ." They both smiled. She felt tenderness for him, and a pride in knowing him.

"Will you be coming in to Kampe, I wonder, when bad weather comes?"

"I don't know how the roads will be."

"If you do, come by," he said. "If you like."

"I will."

They noticed then that Stefan was gone.

"I don't know where he went to," Kostant said. "He comes and he goes, Stefan does. Your brother, Martin, they tell me he's a good lad in our crew."

"He's young," Ekata said.

"It's hard at first. I went in at fifteen. But then when you've got your strength, you know the work, and it goes easy. Good wishes to your family, then." She shook his big, hard, warm hand, and let herself out. On the doorstep she met Stefan face to face. He turned red. It shocked her to see a man blush. He spoke, as usual leaping straight into the subject—"You were the year behind me in school, weren't you?"

"Yes."

"You went around with Rosa Bayenin. She won the scholarship I did, the next year."

"She's teaching school now, in the Valone."

"She did more with it than I would have done. —I was thinking, see, it's queer how you grow up in a place like this, you know everybody, then you meet one and find out you don't know them."

She did not know what to answer. He said good-bye and went into the house; she went on, retying her kerchief against the rising wind.

Rosana and the mother came into the house a minute after Stefan. "Who was that on the doorstep you were talking to?" the mother said sharply. "That wasn't Nona Katalny, I'll be bound."

"You're right," Stefan said.

"All right, but you watch out for that one, you're just the kind she'd like to get her claws into, and wouldn't that be fine, you could walk her puppydog whilst she entertains her ma's gentlemen boarders." She and Rosana both began to laugh their loud, dark laughter. "Who was it you were talking to, then?"

"What's it to you?" he shouted back. Their laughter enraged him; it was like a pelting with hard clattering rocks, too thick to dodge.

"What is it to me who's standing on my own doorstep, you want to know, I'll let you know what it is to me—" Words leapt to meet her anger as they did to all her passions. "You so high and mighty all the time with all your going off to college, but you came sneaking back quick enough to this house, didn't you, and I'll let you know I want to know who comes into this house—" Rosana was shouting, "I know who it was, it was Martin Sachik's sister!" Kostant loomed up suddenly beside the three of them, stooped and tall on his crutches: "Cut it out," he said, and they fell silent.

Nothing was said, then or later, to the mother or between the two brothers, about Ekata Sachik's having been in the house.

Martin took his sister to dine at the Bell, the café where officials of the Chorin Company and visitors from out of town went to dine. He was proud of himself for having thought of treating her, proud of the white tablecloths and the forks and soupspoons, terrified of the waiter. He in his outgrown Sunday coat and his sister in her grey dress, how admirably they were behaving, how adult they were. Ekata looked at the menu so calmly, and her face did not change expression in the slightest as she murmured to him, "But there's two kinds of soup."

"Yes," he said, with sophistication.

"Do you choose which kind?"

"I guess so."

"You must, you'd bloat up before you ever got to the meat—" They snickered. Ekata's shoulders shook; she hid her face in her napkin; the napkin was enormous—"Martin, look, they've given me a bedsheet—" They both sat snorting, shaking, in torment, while the waiter, with another bedsheet on his shoulder, inexorably approached.

Dinner was ordered inaudibly, eaten with etiquette, elbows pressed close to the sides. The dessert was a chestnut-flour pudding, and Ekata, her elbows relaxing a little with enjoyment, said, "Rosa Bayenin said when she wrote the town she's in is right next to a whole forest of chestnut trees, everybody goes and picks them up in autumn, the trees grow thick as night, she said, right down to the river bank." Town after six weeks on the farm, the talk with Kostant and Stefan, dining at the restaurant had excited her. "This is awfully good," she said, but she could not say what she saw, which was sunlight striking golden down a river between endless dark-foliaged trees, a wind running upriver among shadows and the scent of leaves, of water, and of chestnut-flour pudding, a world of forests, of rivers, of strangers, the sunlight shining on the world.

"Saw you talking with Stefan Fabbre," Martin said.

"I was at their house."

"What for?"

"They asked me."

"What for?"

"Just to find out how we're getting on."

"They never asked me."

"You're not on the farm, stupid. You're in his crew, aren't you? You could look in sometime, you know. He's a grand man, you'd like him."

Martin grunted. He resented Ekata's visit to the Fabbres without knowing why. It seemed somehow to complicate things. Rosana had probably been there. He did not want his sister knowing about Rosana. Knowing what about Rosana? He gave it up, scowling.

"The younger brother, Stefan, he works at the Chorin office, doesn't he?"

"Keeps books or something. He was supposed to be a genius and go to college, but they kicked him out."

"I know." She finished her pudding, lovingly. "Everybody knows that," she said.

"I don't like him," Martin said.

"Why not?"

"Just don't." He was relieved, having dumped his ill humor onto Stefan. "You want coffee?"

"Oh, no."

"Come on. I do." Masterful, he ordered coffee for both. Ekata admired him, and enjoyed the coffee. "What luck, to have a brother," she said. The next morning, Sunday, Martin met her at the hotel and they went to church; singing the Lutheran hymns each heard the other's strong clear voice and each was pleased and wanted to laugh. Stefan Fabbre was at the service. "Does he usually come?" Ekata asked Martin as they left the church.

"No," Martin said, though he had no idea, having not been to church himself since May. He felt dull and fierce after the long sermon. "He's following you around."

She said nothing.

"He waited for you at the hotel, you said. Takes you out to see his brother, he says. Talks to you on the street. Shows up in church." Self-defense furnished him these items one after another, and the speaking of them convinced him.

"Martin," Ekata said, "if there's one kind of man I hate it's a meddler."

"If you weren't my sister—"

"If I wasn't your sister I'd be spared your stupidness. Will you go ask the man to put the horse in?" So they parted with mild rancor between them, soon lost in distance and the days.

In late November when Ekata drove in again to Sfaroy Kampe she went to the Fabbre house. She wanted to go, and had told Kostant she would, yet she had to force herself; and when she found that Kostant and Rosana were home, but Stefan was not, she felt much easier. Martin had troubled her with his stupid meddling. It was Kostant she wanted to see, anyhow.

But Kostant wanted to talk about Stefan.

"He's always out roaming, or at the Lion. Restless. Wastes his time. He said to me, one day we talked, he's afraid to leave Kampe. I've thought about what he meant. What is it he's afraid of?"

"Well, he hasn't any friends but here."

"Few enough here. He acts the clerk among the quarrymen, and the quarryman among the clerks. I've seen him, here, when my mates come in. Why don't he be what he is?"

"Maybe he isn't sure what he is."

"He won't learn it from mooning around and drinking at the Lion," said Kostant, hard and sure in his own intactness. "And rubbing up quarrels. He's had three fights this month. Lost 'em all, poor devil," and he laughed. She never expected the innocence of laughter on his grave face. And he was kind; his concern for Stefan was deep, his laughter without a sneer, the laughter of a good nature. Like Stefan, she wondered at him, at his beauty and his strength, but she did not think of him as wasted. The Lord keeps the house and knows his servants. If he had sent this innocent and splendid man to live obscure on the plain of stone, it was part of his housekeeping, of the strange economy of the stone and the rose, the rivers that run and do not run dry, the tiger, the ocean, the maggot, and the not eternal stars.

Rosana, by the hearth, listened to them talk. She sat silent, heavy and her shoulders stooped, though of late she had been learning again to hold herself erect as she had when she was a child, a year ago. They say one gets used to being a millionaire; so after a year or two a human being begins to get used to being a woman. Rosana was learning to wear the rich and heavy garment of her inheritance. Just now she was listening, something she had rarely done. She had never heard adults talk as these two were talking. She had never heard a conversation. At the end of twenty minutes she slipped quietly out. She had learned enough, too much, she needed time to absorb and practice. She began practicing at once. She went down the street erect, not slow and not fast, her face composed, like Ekata Sachik.

"Daydreaming, Ros?" jeered Martin Sachik from the Katalny yard.

She smiled at him and said, "Hello, Martin." He stood staring.

"Where you going?" he asked with caution.

"Nowhere; I'm just walking. Your sister's at our house."

"She is?" Martin sounded unusually stupid and belligerent, but she stuck to her practicing: "Yes," she said politely. "She came to see my brother."

"Which brother?"

"Kostant, why would she have to come see Stefan?" she said, forgetting her new self a moment and grinning widely.

"How come you're barging around all by yourself?"

"Why not?" she said, stung by "barging" and so reverting to an extreme mildness of tone.

"I'll go with you."

"Why not?"

They walked down Gulhelm Street till it became a track between weeds.

"Want to go on to the West Pit?"

"Why not?" Rosana liked the phrase; it sounded experienced.

They walked on the thin stony dirt between miles of dead grass too short to bow to the northwest wind. Enormous masses of cloud travelled backward over their heads so that they seemed to be walking very fast, the grey plain sliding along with them. "Clouds make you dizzy," Martin said, "like looking up a flagpole." They walked with faces upturned, seeing nothing but the motion of the wind. Rosana realised that though their feet were on the earth they themselves stuck up into the sky, it was the sky they were walking through, just as birds flew through it. She looked over at Martin walking through the sky.

They came to the abandoned quarry and stood looking down at the water, dulled by flurries of trapped wind.

"Want to go swimming?"

"Why not?"

"There's the mule trail. Looks funny, don't it, going right down into the water."

"It's cold here."

"Come on down the trail. There's no wind inside the walls hardly. That's where Penik jumped off from, they grappled him up from right under here."

Rosana stood on the lip of the pit. The grey wind blew by her. "Do you think he meant to? I mean, he was blind, maybe he fell in—"

"He could see some. They were going to send him to Brailava and operate on him. Come on." She followed him to the beginning of the path down. It looked very steep from above. She had become timorous the last year. She followed him slowly down the effaced, boulder-smashed track into the quarry. "Here, hold on," he said, pausing at a rough drop; he took her hand and brought her down after him. They separated at once and he led on to where the water cut across the path, which plunged on down to the hidden floor of the quarry. The water was lead-dark, uneasy, its surface broken into thousands of tiny pleatings, circles, counter-circles by the faint trapped wind jarring it ceaselessly against the walls. "Shall I go on?" Martin whispered, loud in the silence.

"Why not?"

He walked on. She cried, "Stop!" He had walked into the water up to his knees; he turned, lost his balance, careened back onto the path with a plunge that showered her with water and sent clapping echoes round the walls of rock. "You're crazy, what did you do that for?" Martin sat down, took off his big shoes to dump water out of them, and laughed, a soundless laugh mixed with shivering. "What did you do that for?"

"Felt like it," he said. He caught at her arm, pulled her down kneeling by him, and kissed her. The kiss went on. She began to struggle, and pulled away from him. He hardly knew it. He lay there on the rocks at the water's edge laughing; he was as strong as the earth and could not lift his hand. . . . He sat up, mouth open, eyes unfocussed. After a while he put on his wet, heavy shoes and started up the path. She stood at the top, a windblown stroke of darkness against the huge moving sky. "Come on!" she shouted, and wind thinned her voice to a knife's edge. "Come on, you can't catch me!" As he neared the top of the path, she ran. He ran, weighed down by his wet shoes and trousers. A hundred yards from the quarry he caught her and tried to capture both her arms. Her wild face was next to his for a moment. She twisted free, ran off again, and he followed her into town, trotting since he could not run any more. Where Gulhelm Street began she stopped and waited for him. They walked down the pavement side by side. "You look like a drowned cat," she jeered in a panting whisper. "Who's talking," he answered the same way, "look at the mud on your skirt." In front of the boarding house they stopped and looked at each other, and he laughed. "Good night, Ros!" he said. She wanted to bite him. "Good night!" she said, and walked the few yards to her own front door, not slow and not fast, feeling his gaze on her back like a hand on her flesh.

Not finding her brother at the boarding house, Ekata had gone back to the hotel to wait for him; they were to dine at the Bell again. She told the desk clerk to send her brother up when he came. In a few minutes there was a knock; she opened the door. It was Stefan Fabbre. He was the color of oatmeal and looked dingy, like an unmade bed.

"I wanted to ask you . . ." His voice slurred off. "Have some dinner," he muttered, looking past her at the room.

"My brother's coming for me. That's him now." But it was the hotel manager coming up the stairs. "Sorry, miss," he said loudly. "There's a parlour downstairs." Ekata stared at him blankly. "Now look, miss, you said to send up your brother, and the clerk he don't know your brother by sight, but I do. That's my business. There's a nice parlour downstairs for entertaining. All right? You want to come to a respectable hotel, I want to keep it respectable for you, see?"

Stefan pushed past him and blundered down the stairs. "He's drunk, miss," said the manager.

"Go away," Ekata said, and shut the door on him. She sat down on the bed with clenched hands, but she could not sit still. She jumped up, took up her coat and kerchief, and without putting them on ran downstairs and out, hurling the key onto the desk behind which the manager stood staring. Ardure Street was dark between pools of lamplight, and the winter wind blew down it. She walked the two blocks west, came back down the other side of the street the length of it, eight blocks; she passed the White Lion, but the winter door was up and she could not see in. It was cold, the wind ran through the streets like a river running. She went to Gulhelm Street and met Martin coming out of the boarding house. They went to the Bell for supper. Both were thoughtful and uneasy. They spoke little and gently, grateful for companionship.

Alone in church next morning, when she had made sure that Stefan was not there, she lowered her eyes in relief. The stone walls of the church and the stark words of the service stood strong around her. She rested like a ship in haven. Then as the pastor gave his text, "I will lift up mine eyes unto the hills, whence cometh my help," she shivered, and once again looked all about the church, moving her head and eyes slowly, surreptitiously, seeking him. She heard nothing of the sermon. But when the service was over she did not want to leave the church. She went out among the last of the congregation. The pastor detained her, asking about her mother. She saw Stefan waiting at the foot of the steps.

She went to him.

"Wanted to apologise for last night," he brought out all in one piece.

"It's all right."

He was bareheaded and the wind blew his light, dusty-looking hair across his eyes; he winced and tried to smooth it back. "I was drunk," he said.

"I know."

They set off together.

"I was worried about you," Ekata said.

"What for? I wasn't that drunk."

"I don't know."

They crossed the street in silence.

"Kostant likes talking with you. Told me so." His tone was unpleasant. Ekata said drily, "I like talking with him."

"Everybody does. It's a great favor he does them."

She did not reply.

"I mean that."

She knew what he meant, but still did not say anything. They were near the hotel. He stopped. "I won't finish ruining your reputation."

"You don't have to grin about it."

"I'm not. I mean I won't go on to the hotel with you, in case it embarrassed you."

"I have nothing to be embarrassed about."

"I do, and I am. I am sorry, Ekata."

"I didn't mean you had to apologise again." Her voice turned husky so that he thought again of mist, dusk, the forests.

"I won't." He laughed. "Are you leaving right away?"

"I have to. It gets dark so early now."

They both hesitated.

"You could do me a favor," she said.

"I'd do that."

"If you'd see to having my horse put in, last time I had to stop after a mile and tighten everything. If you did that I could be getting ready."

When she came out of the hotel the wagon was out front and he was in the seat. "I'll drive you a mile or two, all right?" She nodded, he gave her a hand up; they drove down Ardure Street westward to the plain.

"That damned hotel manager," Ekata said. "Grinning and scraping this morning . . ."

Stefan laughed, but said nothing. He was cautious, absorbed; the cold wind blew, the old roan clopped along; he explained presently, "I've never driven before."

"I've never driven any horse but this one. He's never any trouble."

The wind whistled in miles of dead grass, tugged at her black kerchief, whipped Stefan's hair across his eyes.

"Look at it," he said softly. "A couple of inches of dirt, and under it rock. Drive all day, any direction, and you'll find rock, with a couple of inches of dirt on it. You know how many trees there are in Kampe? Fifty-four. I counted 'em. And not another, not one, all the way to the mountains." His voice as he talked as if to himself was dry and musical. "When I went to Brailava on the train I looked out for the first new tree. The fifty-fifth tree. It was a big oak by a farmhouse in the hills. Then all of a sudden there were trees everywhere, in all the valleys in the hills. You could never count 'em. But I'd like to try."

"You're sick of it here."

"I don't know. Sick of something. I feel like I was an ant, something smaller, so small you can hardly see it, crawling along on this huge floor. Getting nowhere because where is there to get. Look at us now, crawling across the floor, there's the ceiling. . . . Looks like snow, there in the north."

"Not before dark, I hope."

"What's it like on the farm?"

She considered some while before answering, and then said softly, "Closed in."

"Your father happy with it?"

"He never did feel easy in Kampe, I think."

"There's people made out of dirt, earth," he said in his voice that slurred away so easily into unheard monologue, "and then there's some made out of stone. The fellows who get on in Kampe are made out of stone." "Like my brother," he did not say, and she heard it.

"Why don't you leave?"

"That's what Kostant said. It sounds so easy. But see, if he left, he'd be taking himself with him. I'd be taking myself. . . . Does it matter where you go? All you have is what you are. Or what you meet."

He checked the horse. "I'd better hop off, we must have come a couple of miles. Look, there's the antheap." From the high wagon seat looking back they saw a darkness on the pale plain, a pinpoint spire, a glitter where the winter sun struck windows or roof-slates; and far behind the town, distinct under high, heavy, dark-grey clouds, the mountains.

He handed the traces to her. "Thanks for the lift," he said, and swung down from the seat.

"Thanks for the company, Stefan."

He raised his hand; she drove on. It seemed a cruel thing to do, to leave him on foot there on the plain. When she looked back she saw him far behind already, walking away from her between the narrowing wheel-ruts under the enormous sky.

Before she reached the farm that evening there was a dry flurry of snow, the first of an early winter. From the kitchen window all that month she looked up at hills blurred with rain. In December from her bedroom, on days of sun after snow, she saw eastward across the plain a glittering pallor: the mountains. There were no more trips to Sfaroy Kampe. When they needed market goods her uncle drove to Verre or Lotima, bleak villages foundering like cardboard in the rain. It was too easy to stray off the wheel-ruts crossing the karst in snow or heavy rain, he said, "and then where are ye?"

"Where are ye in the first place?" Ekata answered in Stefan's soft dry voice. The uncle paid no heed.

Martin rode out on a livery-stable horse for Christmas day. After a few hours he got sullen and stuck to Ekata. "What's that thing Aunt's got hanging round her neck?"

"A nail through an onion. To keep off rheumatism."

"Christ Almighty!"

Ekata laughed.

"The whole place stinks of onion and flannel, can't you air it out?"

"No. Cold days they even close the chimney flues. Rather have the smoke than the cold."

"You ought to come back to town with me, Ekata."

"Ma's not well."

"You can't help that."

"No. But I'd feel mean to leave her without good reason. First things first." Ekata had lost weight; her cheekbones stood out and her eyes looked darker. "How's it going with you?" she asked presently.

"All right. We've been laid off a good bit, the snow."

"You've been growing up," Ekata said.

"I know."

He sat on the stiff farm-parlour sofa with a man's weight, a man's quietness.

"You walking out with anybody?"

"No." They both laughed. "Listen, I saw Fabbre, and he said to wish you joy of the season. He's better. Gets outside now, with a cane."

Their cousin came through the room. She wore a man's old boots stuffed with straw for warmth getting about in the ice and mud of the farmyard. Martin looked after her with disgust. "I had a talk with him. Couple of weeks ago. I hope he's back in the pits by Easter like they say. He's my foreman, you know." Looking at him, Ekata saw who it was he was in love with.

"I'm glad you like him."

"There isn't a man in Kampe comes up to his shoulder. You liked him, didn't you?"

"Of course I did."

"See, when he asked about you, I thought—"

"You thought wrong," Ekata said. "Will you quit meddling, Martin?"

"I didn't say anything," he defended himself feebly; his sister could still overawe him. He also recalled that Rosana Fabbre had laughed at him when he had said something to her about Kostant and Ekata. She had been hanging out sheets in the back yard on a whipping-bright winter morning a few days ago, he had hung over the back fence talking to her. "Oh Lord, are you crazy?" she had jeered, while the damp sheets on the line billowed at her face and the wind tangled her hair. "Those two? Not on your life!" He had tried to argue; she would not listen. "He's not going to marry anybody from here. There's going to be some woman from far off, from Krasnoy maybe, a manager's wife, a queen, a beauty, with servants and all. And one day she'll be coming down Ardure Street with her nose in the air and she'll see Kostant coming with his nose in the air, and crack! that's it."

"That's what?" said he, fascinated by her fortune-teller's conviction.

"I don't know!" she said, and hoisted up another sheet. "Maybe they'll run off together. Maybe something else. All I know is Kostant knows what's coming to him, and he's going to wait for it."

"All right, if you know so much, what's coming your way?"

She opened her mouth wide in a big grin, her dark eyes under long dark brows flashed at him. "Men," she said like a cat hissing, and the sheets and shirts snapped and billowed around her, white in the flashing sunlight.

January passed, covering the surly plain with snow, February with a grey sky moving slowly over the plain from north to south day after day: a hard winter and a long one. Kostant Fabbre got a lift sometimes on a cart to the Chorin quarries north of town, and would stand watching the work, the teams of men and lines of wagons, the shunting boxcars, the white of snow and the dull white of new-cut limestone. Men would come up to the tall man leaning on his cane to ask him how he did, when he was coming back to work. "A few weeks yet," he would say. The company was keeping him laid off till April as their insurers requested. He felt fit, he could walk back to town without using his cane, it fretted him bitterly to be idle. He would go back, to the White Lion, and sit there in the smoky dark and warmth till the quarrymen came in, off work at four because of snow and darkness, big heavy men making the place steam with the heat of their bodies and buzz with the mutter of their voices. At five Stefan would come in, slight, with white shirt and light shoes, a queer figure among the quarriers. He usually came to Kostant's table, but they were not on good terms. Each was waiting and impatient.

"Evening," Martin Sachik said passing the table, a tired burly lad, smiling. "Evening, Stefan."

"I'm Fabbre and Mr to you, laddie," Stefan said in his soft voice that yet stood out against the comfortable hive-mutter. Martin, already past, chose to pay no attention.

"Why are you down on that one?"

"Because I don't choose to be on first names with every man's brat that goes down in the pits. Nor every man either. D'you take me for the town idiot?"

"You act like it, times," Kostant said, draining his beermug.

"I've had enough of your advice."

"I've had enough of your conceit. Go to the Bell if the company here don't suit you."

Stefan got up, slapped money on the table, and went out.

It was the first of March; the north half of the sky over the streets was heavy, without light; its edge was silvery blue, and from it south to the horizon the air was blue and empty except for a fingernail moon over the western hills and, near it, the evening star. Stefan went silent through the streets, a silent wind at his back. Indoors, the walls of the house enclosed his rage; it became a square, dark, musty thing full of the angles of tables and chairs, and flared up yellow with the kerosene lamp. The chimney of the lamp slithered out of his hand like a live animal, smashed itself shrilly against the corner of the table. He was on all fours picking up bits of glass when his brother came in.

"What did you follow me for?"

"I came to my own house."

"Do I have to go back to the Lion then?"

"Go where you damned well like." Kostant sat down and picked up yesterday's newspaper. Stefan, kneeling, broken glass on the palm of his hand, spoke: "Listen. I know why you want me patting young Sachik on the head. For one thing he thinks you're God Almighty, and that's agreeable. For another thing he's got a sister. And you want 'em all eating out of your hand, don't you? Like they all do? Well by God here's one that won't, and you might find your game spoiled, too." He got up and went to the kitchen, to the trash basket that stood by the week's heap of dirty clothes, and dropped the glass of the broken lamp into the basket. He stood looking at his hand: a sliver of glass bristled from the inner joint of his second finger. He had clenched his hand on the glass as he spoke to Kostant. He pulled out the sliver and put the bleeding finger to his mouth. Kostant came in. "What game, Stefan?" he said.

"You know what I mean."

"Say what you mean."

"I mean her. Ekata. What do you want her for anyhow? You don't need her. You don't need anything. You're the big tin god."

"You shut your mouth."

"Don't give me orders! By God I can give orders too. You just stay away from her. I'll get her and you won't, I'll get her under your nose, under your eyes—" Kostant's big hands took hold of his shoulders and shook him till his head snapped back and forth on his neck. He broke free and drove his fist straight at Kostant's face, but as he did so he felt a jolt as when a train-car is coupled to the train. He fell down backwards across the heap of dirty clothes. His head hit the floor with a dead sound like a dropped melon.

Kostant stood with his back against the stove. He looked at his right-hand knuckles, then at Stefan's face, which was dead white and curiously serene. Kostant took a pillowcase from the pile of clothes, wet it at the sink, and knelt down by Stefan. It was hard for him to kneel, the right leg was still stiff. He mopped away the thin dark line of blood that had run from Stefan's mouth. Stefan's face twitched, he sighed and blinked, and looked up at Kostant, gazing with vague, sliding recognition, like a young infant.

"That's better," Kostant said. His own face was white.

Stefan propped himself up on one arm. "I fell down," he said in a faint, surprised voice. Then he looked at Kostant again and his face began to change and tighten.

"Stefan—"

Stefan got up on all fours, then onto his feet; Kostant tried to take his arm, but he stumbled to the door, struggled with the catch, and plunged out. At the door, Kostant watched him vault the fence, cut across the Katalny yard, and run down Gulhelm Street with long, jolting strides. For several minutes the elder brother stood in the doorway, his face rigid and sorrowful. Then he turned, went to the front door and out, and made off down Gulhelm Street as fast as he could. The black cloud-front had covered all the sky but a thin band of blue-green to the south; the moon and star were gone. Kostant followed the track over the plain to the West Pit. No one was ahead of him. He reached the lip of the quarry and saw the water quiet, dim, reflecting snow that had yet to fall. He called out once, "Stefan!" His lungs were raw and his throat dry from the effort he had made to run. There was no answer. It was not his brother's name that need be called there at the lip of the ruined quarry. It was the wrong name, and the wrong time. Kostant turned and started back towards Gulhelm Street, walking slowly and a little lame.

"I've got to ride to Kolle," Stefan said. The livery-stable keeper stared at his blood-smeared chin.

"It's dark. There's ice on the roads."

"You must have a sharp-shod horse. I'll pay double."

"Well . . ."

Stefan rode out of the stable yard, and turned right down Ardure Street towards Verre instead of left towards Kolle. The keeper shouted after him. Stefan kicked the horse, which fell into a trot and then, where the pavement ceased, into a heavy run. The band of blue-green light in the southwest veered and slid away, Stefan thought he was falling sideways, he clung to the pommel but did not pull the reins. When the horse ran itself out and slowed to a walk it was full night, earth and sky all dark. The horse snorted, the saddle creaked, the wind hissed in frozen grass. Stefan dismounted and searched the ground as best he could. The horse had kept to the wagon road and stood not four feet from the ruts. They went on, horse and man; mounted, the man could not see the ruts; he let the horse follow the track across the plain, himself following no road.

After a long time in the rocking dark something touched his face once, lightly.

He felt his cheek. The right side of his jaw was swollen and stiff, and his right hand holding the reins was locked by the cold so that when he tried to change his grip he did not know if his fingers moved or not. He had no gloves, though he wore the winter coat he had never taken off when he came into the house, when the lamp broke, a long time ago. He got the reins in his left hand and put the right inside his coat to warm it. The horse jogged on patiently, head low. Again something touched Stefan's face very lightly, brushing his cheek, his hot sore lip. He could not see the flakes. They were soft and did not feel cold. He waited for the gentle, random touch of the snow. He changed hands on the reins again, and put the left hand under the horse's coarse, damp mane, on the warm hide. They both took comfort in the touch. Trying to see ahead, Stefan knew where sky and horizon met, or thought he did, but the plain was gone. The ceiling of sky was gone. The horse walked on darkness, under darkness, through darkness.

Once the word "lost" lit itself like a match in the darkness, and Stefan tried to stop the horse so he could get off and search for the wheel-ruts, but the horse kept walking on. Stefan let his numb hand holding the reins rest on the pommel, let himself be borne.

The horse's head came up, its gait changed for a few steps. Stefan clutched at the wet mane, raised his own head dizzily, blinked at a spiderweb of light tangled in his eyes. Through the splintery blur of ice on his lashes the light grew square and yellowish: a window. What house stood out alone here on the endless plain? Dim blocks of pallor rose up on both sides of him—storefronts, a street. He had come to Verre. The horse stopped and sighed so that the girths creaked loudly. Stefan did not remember leaving Sfaroy Kampe. He sat astride a sweating horse in a dark street somewhere. One window was alight in a second storey. Snow fell in sparse clumps, as if hurled down in handfuls. There was little on the ground, it melted as it touched, a spring snow. He rode to the house with the lighted window and called aloud, "Where's the road to Lotima?"

The door opened, snow flickered whirling in the shaft of light. "Are ye the doctor?"

"No. How do I get on to Lotima?"

"Next turn right. If ye meet the doctor tell him hurry on!"

The horse left the village unwillingly, lame on one leg and then the other. Stefan kept his head raised looking for the dawn, which surely must be near. He rode north now, the snow blowing in his face, blinding him even to the darkness. The road climbed, went down, climbed again. The horse stopped, and when Stefan did nothing, turned left, made a couple of stumbling steps, stopped again shuddering and neighed. Stefan dismounted, falling to hands and knees because his legs were too stiff at first to hold him. There was a cattle-guard of poles laid across a side-road. He let the horse stand and felt his way up the side-road to a sudden house lifting a dark wall and snowy roof above him. He found the door, knocked, waited, knocked; a window rattled, a woman said frightened to death over his head, "Who's that?"

"Is this the Sachik farm?"

"No! Who's that?"

"Have I passed the Sachiks'?"

"Are ye the doctor?"

"Yes."

"It's the next but one on the left side. Want a lantern, doctor?"

She came downstairs and gave him a lantern and matches; she held a candle, which dazzled his eyes so that he never saw her face.

He went at the horse's head now, the lantern in his left hand and the reins in his right, held close to the bridle. The horse's docile, patient, stumbling walk, the liquid darkness of its eye in the gleam of the lantern, grieved Stefan sorely. They walked ahead very slowly and he looked for the dawn.

A farmhouse flickered to his left when he was almost past it; snow, wind-plastered on its north wall, caught the light of the lantern. He led the horse back. The hinges of the gate squealed. Dark outbuildings crowded round. He knocked, waited, knocked. A light moved inside the house, the door opened, again a candle held at eye-level dazzled him.

"Who is that?"

"That's you, Ekata," he said.

"Who is that? Stefan?"

"I must have missed the other farm, the one in between."

"Come in—"

"The horse. Is that the stable?"

"There, to the left—"

He was all right while he found a stall for the horse, robbed the Sachiks' roan of some hay and water, found a sack and rubbed the horse down a bit; he did all that very well, he thought, but when he got back to the house his knees went weak and he could scarcely see the room or Ekata who took his hand to bring him in. She had on a coat over something white, a nightgown. "Oh lad," she said, "you rode from Kampe tonight?"

"Poor old horse," he said, and smiled. His voice said the words some while after he thought he had said them. He sat down on the sofa.

"Wait there," she said. It seemed she left the room for a while, then she was putting a cup of something in his hands. He drank; it was hot; the sting of brandy woke him long enough to watch her stir up the buried coals and put wood on the fire. "I wanted to talk to you, see," he said, and then he fell asleep.

She took off his shoes, put his legs up on the sofa, got a blanket and put it over him, tended the reluctant fire. He never stirred. She turned out the lamp and slipped back upstairs in the dark. Her bed was by the window of her attic room, and she could see or feel that it was now snowing soft and thick in the dark outside.

She roused to a knock and sat up seeing the even light of snow on walls and ceiling. Her uncle peered in. He was wearing yellowish-white woollen underwear and his hair stuck up like fine wire around his bald spot. The whites of his eyes were the same color as his underwear. "Who's that downstairs?"

Ekata explained to Stefan, somewhat later in the morning, that he was on his way to Lotima on business for the Chorin Company, that he had started from Kampe at noon and been held up by a stone in his horse's shoe and then by the snow.

"Why?" he said, evidently confused, his face looking rather childish with fatigue and sleep.

"I had to tell them something."

He scratched his head. "What time did I get here?"

"About two in the morning."

He remembered how he had looked for the dawn, hours away.

"What did you come for?" Ekata said. She was clearing the breakfast table; her face was stern, though she spoke softly.

"I had a fight," Stefan said. "With Kostant."

She stopped, holding two plates, and looked at him.

"You don't think I hurt him?" He laughed. He was light-headed, tired out, serene. "He knocked me cold. You don't think I could have beat him?"

"I don't know," Ekata said with distress.

"I always lose fights," Stefan said. "And run away."

The deaf man came through, dressed to go outside in heavy boots, an old coat made of blanketing; it was still snowing. "Ye'll not get on to Lotima today, Mr Stefan," he said in his loud even voice, with satisfaction. "Tomas says the nag's lame on four legs." This had been discussed at breakfast, but the deaf man had not heard. He had not asked how Kostant was getting on, and when he did so later in the day it was with the same satisfied malice: "And your brother, he's down in the pits again, no doubt?" He did not try to hear the answer.

Stefan spent most of the day by the fire sleeping. Only Ekata's cousin was curious about him. She said to Ekata as they were cooking supper, "They say his brother is a handsome man."

"Kostant? The handsomest man I ever saw." Ekata smiled, chopping onions.

"I don't know as I'd call this one handsome," the cousin said tentatively.

The onions were making Ekata cry; she laughed, blew her nose, shook her head. "Oh no," she said.

After supper Stefan met Ekata as she came into the kitchen from dumping out peelings and swill for the pigs. She wore her father's coat, clogs on her shoes, her black kerchief. The freezing wind swept in with her till she wrestled the door shut. "It's clearing," she said, "the wind's from the south."

"Ekata, do you know what I came here for—"

"Do you know yourself?" she said, looking up at him as she set the bucket down.

"Yes, I do."

"Then I do, I suppose."

"There isn't anywhere," he said in rage as the uncle's clumping boots approached the kitchen.

"There's my room," she said impatiently. But the walls were

thin, and the cousin slept in the next attic and her parents across the stairwell; she frowned angrily and said, "No. Wait till the morning."

In the morning, early, the cousin went off alone down the road. She was back in half an hour, her straw-stuffed boots smacking in the thawing snow and mud. The neighbor's wife at the next house but one had said, "He said he was the doctor, I asked who it was was sick with you. I gave him the lantern, it was so dark I didn't see his face, I thought it was the doctor, he said so." The cousin was munching the words sweetly, deciding whether to accost Stefan with them, or Ekata, or both before witnesses, when around a bend and down the snow-clotted, sun-bright grade of the road two horses came at a long trot: the livery-stable horse and the farm's old roan. Stefan and Ekata rode; they were both laughing. "Where ye going?" the cousin shouted, trembling. "Running away," the young man called back, and they went past her, splashing the puddles into diamond-slivers in the sunlight of March, and were gone.

1910

A Week in the Country

On a sunny morning of 1962 in Cleveland, Ohio, it was raining in Krasnoy and the streets between grey walls were full of men. "It's raining down my neck in here," Kasimir complained, but his friend in the adjoining stall of the streetcorner W.C. did not hear him because he was also talking: "Historical necessity is a solecism, what is history except what had to happen? But you can't extend that. What happens next? God knows!" Kasimir followed him out, still buttoning his trousers, and looked at the small boy looking at the nine-foot-long black coffin leaning against the W.C. "What's in it?" the boy asked. "My great-aunt's body," Kasimir explained. He picked up the coffin, hurried on with Stefan Fabbre through the rain. "A farce, determinism's a farce. Anything to avoid awe. Show me a seed," Stefan Fabbre said stopping and pointing at Kasimir, "yes, I can tell you what it is, it's an apple seed. But can I tell you that an apple tree will grow from it? No! Because there's no freedom, we think there's a law. But there is no law. There's growth and death, delight and terror, an abyss, the rest we invent. We're going to miss the train." They jostled on up Tiypontiy Street, the rain fell harder. Stefan Fabbre strode swinging his briefcase, his mouth firmly closed, his white face shining wet. "Why didn't you take up the piccolo? Give me that awhile," he said as Kasimir tangled with an office-worker running for a bus. "Science bearing the burden of Art," Kasimir said, "heavy, isn't it?" as his friend hoisted the case and lugged it on, frowning and by the time they reached West Station gasping. On the platform in rain and steam they ran as others ran, heard whistles shriek and urgent Sanskrit blare from loudspeakers, and lurched exhausted into the first car. The compartments were all empty. It was the other train that was pulling out, jammed, a suburban train. Theirs sat still for ten minutes. "Nobody on this train but us?" Stefan Fabbre asked, morose, standing at the window. Then with one high peep the walls slid away. Raindrops shook and merged on the pane, tracks interwove on a viaduct, the two young men stared into bedroom windows and at brick walls painted with enormous letters. Abruptly nothing was left in the rain-dark evening sliding backwards to the east but a line of hills, black against a colorless clearing sky.

"The country," Stefan Fabbre said.

He got out a biochemical journal from amongst socks and undershirts in his briefcase, put on dark-rimmed glasses, read. Kasimir pushed back wet hair that had fallen all over his forehead, read the sign on the windowsill that said DO NOT LEAN OUT, stared at the shaking walls and the rain shuddering on the window, dozed. He dreamed that walls were falling down around him. He woke scared as they pulled out of Okats. His friend sat looking out the window, white-faced and black-haired, confirming the isolation and disaster of Kasimir's dream. "Can't see anything," he said. "Night. Country's the only place where they have night left." He stared through the reflection of his own face into the night that filled his eyes with blessed darkness.

"So here we are on a train going to Aisnar," Kasimir said, "but we don't know that it's going to Aisnar. It might go to Peking."

"It might derail and we'll all be killed. And if we do come to Aisnar? What's Aisnar? Mere hearsay." — "That's morbid," Kasimir said, glimpsing again the walls collapsing. — "No, exhilarating," his friend answered. "Takes a lot of work to hold the world together, when you look at it that way. But it's worthwhile. Building up cities, holding up the roofs by an act of fidelity. Not faith. Fidelity." He gazed out the window through his reflected eyes. Kasimir shared a bar of mud-like chocolate with him. They came to Aisnar.

Rain fell in the gold-paved, ill-lit streets while the autobus to Vermare and Prevne waited for its passengers in South Square under dripping sycamores. The case rode in the back seat. A chicken with a string round its neck scratched the aisle for grain, a bushy-haired woman held the other end of the string, a drunk farm-worker talked loudly to the driver as the bus groaned out of Aisnar southward into the country night, the same night, the blessed darkness.

"So I says to him, I says, you don't know what'll happen tomorrow—"

"Listen," said Kasimir, "if the universe is infinite, does that mean that everything that could possibly happen, is happening, somewhere, at some time?"

"Saturday, he says, Saturday."

"I don't know. It would. But we don't know what's possible. Thank God. If we did, I'd shoot myself, eh?"

"Come back Saturday, he says, and I says, Saturday be damned, I says."

In Vermare rain fell on the ruins of the Tower Keep, and the drunk got off leaving silence behind him. Stefan Fabbre looked glum, said he had a sore throat, and fell into a quick, weary sleep. His head jiggled to the ruts and bumps of the foothill road as the bus ran westward clearing a tunnel through solid black with its headlights. A tree, a great oak, bent down suddenly to shelter it. The doors opened admitting clean air, flashlights, boots and caps. Brushing back his fair hair Kasimir said softly, "Always happens. Only six miles from the border here." They felt in their breast-pockets, handed over. "Fabbre Stefan, domicile 136 Tome Street, Krasnoy, student, MR 64100282A. Augeskar Kasimir, domicile 4 Sorden Street, Krasnoy, student, MR 80104944A. Where are you going?" — "Prevne." — "Both of you? Business?" — "Vacation. A week in the country." — "What's that?" — "A bass-viol case."

— "What's in it?" — "A bass viol." It was stood up, opened, closed again, lugged out, laid on the ground, opened again, and the huge viol stood fragile and magnificent among flashlights over the mud, boots, belt-buckles, caps. "Keep it off the ground!" Kasimir said in a sharp voice, and Stefan pushed in front of him. They fingered it, shook it. "Here, Kasi, does this unscrew? — No, there's no way to take it apart." The fat one slapped the great shining curve of wood saying something about his wife so that Stefan laughed, but the viol tilted in another's hands, a tuning-peg squawked, and on the patter of rain and mutter of the bus-engine idling, a booming twang uncurled, broken off short like the viol-string. Stefan took hold of Kasimir's arm. After the bus had started again they sat side by side in the warm stinking darkness. Kasimir said, "Sorry, Stefan. Thanks."

"Can you fix it?"

"Yes, just the peg snapped. I can fix it."

"Damn sore throat." Stefan rubbed his head and left his hands over his eyes. "Taking cold. Damn rain."

"We're near Prevne now."

In Prevne very fine rain drifted down one street between two streetlamps. Behind the roofs something loomed—treetops, hills? No one met them since Kasimir had forgotten to write which night they were coming. Returning from the one public telephone, he joined Stefan and the bass-viol case at a table of the Post-Telephone Bar. "Father has the car out on a call. We can walk or wait here. Sorry." His long fair face was discouraged, contrite. "It's a couple of miles." They set off. They walked in silence up a dirt road in rain and darkness between fields. The air smelt of wet earth. Kasimir began to whistle but the rain wet his lips, he stopped. It was so dark that they walked slowly, not able to see where each step took them, whether the road was rough or plain. It was so still that they heard the multitudinous whisper of the rain on fields to left and right. They were climbing. The hill loomed ahead of them, solider darkness. Stefan stopped to turn up his wet coatcollar and because he was dizzy. As he went forward again in the chill whispering country silence he heard a soft clear sound, a girl laughing behind the hill. Lights sprang up at the hillcrest, sparkling, waving. "What's that?" he said stopping unnerved in the broken dark. A child shouted, "There they are!" The lights above them danced and descended, they were encircled by lanterns, flashlights, voices calling, faces and arms lit by flashes and vanishing again into night; clearly once more, right at his side, the sweet laugh rang out. "Father didn't come back and you didn't come, so we all came to meet you." — "Did you bring your friend, where is he?" — "Hello, Kasi!" Kasimir's fair head bent to another in the gleam of a lantern. "Where's your fiddle, didn't you bring it?" — "It's been raining like this all week." — "Left it with Mr Praspayets at the Post-Telephone." — "Let's go on and get it, it's lovely walking." — "I'm Bendika, are you Stefan?" She laughed as they sought each other's hands to shake in darkness; she turned her lantern round and was dark-haired, as tall as her brother, the only one of them he saw clearly before they all went back down the road talking, laughing, flashing lightbeams over the road and roadside weeds or up into the rain-thick air. He saw them all for a moment in the bar as Kasimir got his bull-fiddle: two boys, a man, tall Bendika, the young blonde one who had kissed Kasimir, another still younger, all of them he saw all at once and then they were off up the road again and he must wonder which of the three girls, or was it four, had laughed before they met. The chill rain picked at his hot face. Beside him, beaming a flashlight so they could see the road, the man said, "I'm Joachim Bret." — "Enzymes," Stefan replied hoarsely. — "Yes, what's your field?" — "Molecular genetics." — "No! too good! you work with Metor, then? Catch me up, will you? Do you see the American journals?" They talked helices for half a mile, Bret voluble, Stefan laconic as he was still dizzy and still listened for the laugh; but all of them laughed, he could not be sure. They all fell silent a moment, only the two boys ran far ahead, calling. "There's the house," tall Bendika said beside him, pointing to a yellow gleam. "Still with us, Stefan?" Kasimir called from somewhere in the dark. He growled yes, resenting the silly good cheer, the running and calling and laughing, the enthusiastic jerky Bret, the yellow windows that to all of them were home but to him not. Inside the house they shed wet coats, spread, multiplied, regathered around a table in a high dark room shot through with noise and lamplight, for coffee and coffeecake borne in by Kasimir's mother. She walked hurried and tranquil under a grey and dark-brown coronet of braids. Bass-viol-shaped, mother of seven, she merged Stefan with all the other young people whom she distinguished one from another only by name. They were named Valeria, Bendika, Antony, Bruna, Kasimir, Joachim, Paul. They joked and chattered, the little dark girl screamed with laughter, Kasimir's fair hair fell over his eyes, the two boys of eleven squabbled, the gaunt smiling man sat with a guitar and presently played, his face beaked like a crow's over the instrument. His right hand plucking the strings was slightly crippled or deformed. They sang, all but Stefan who did not know the songs, had a sore throat, would not sing, sat rancorous amid the singers. Dr Augeskar came in. He shook Kasimir's hand, welcoming and effacing him, a tall king with a slender and unlikely heir. "Where's your friend? Sorry I couldn't meet you, had an emergency up the road. Appendectomy on the dining table. Like carving the Christmas goose. Get to bed, Antony. Bendika, get me a glass. Joachim? You, Fabbre?" He poured out red wine and sat down with them at the great round table. They sang again. Augeskar suggested the songs, his voice led the others; he filled the room. The fair daughter flirted with him, the little dark one screeched with laughter, Bendika teased Kasimir, Bret sang a love-song in Swedish; it was only eleven o'clock. Dr Augeskar had grey eyes, clear under blond brows. Stefan met their stare. "You've got a cold?" — "Yes." — "Then go to bed. Diana! where does Fabbre sleep?" Kasimir jumped up contrite, led Stefan upstairs and through corridors and rooms all smelling of hay and rain. "When's breakfast?" — "Oh, anytime," for Kasimir never knew the time of any event. "Good night, Stefan." But it was a bad night, miserable, and all through it Bret's crippled hand snapped off one great coiling string after another with a booming twang while he explained, "This is how you go after them the latest," grinning. In the morning Stefan could not get up. Sunlit walls leaned inward over the bed and the sky came stretching in the windows, a huge blue balloon. He lay there. He hid his pin-stiff aching black hair under his hands and moaned. The tall golden-grey man came in and said to him with perfect certainty, "My boy, you're sick." It was balm. Sick, he was sick, the walls and sky were all right. "A very respectable fever you're running," said the doctor and Stefan smiled, near tears, feeling himself respectable, lapped in the broad indifferent tenderness of the big man who was kingly, certain, uncaring as sunlight in the sky. But in the forests and caves and small crowded rooms of his fever no sunlight came, and after a time no water.

The house stood quiet in the September sunlight and dark.

That night Mrs Augeskar, yarn, needle, sock poised one moment in her hands, lifted her braid-crowned head, listening as she had listened years ago to her first son, Kasimir, crying out in sleep in his crib upstairs. "Poor child," she whispered. And Bruna raised her fair head listening too, for the first time, hearing the solitary cry from the forests where she had never been. The house stood still around them. On the second day the boys played outdoors till rain fell and night fell. Kasimir stood in the kitchen sawing on his bull-fiddle, his face by the shining neck of the instrument quiet and closed, keeping right on when others came in to perch on stools and lean against the sink and talk, for after all there were seven young people there on vacation, they could not stay silent. But under their voices the deep, weak, singing voice of Kasimir's fiddle went on wordless, like a cry from the depths of the forest; so that Bruna suddenly past patience and dependence, solitary, not the third daughter and fourth child and one of the young people, slipped away and went upstairs to see what it was like, this grave sickness, this mortality.

It was not like anything. The young man slept. His face was white, his hair black on white linen: clear as printed words, but in a foreign language.

She came down and told her mother she had looked in, he was sleeping quietly; true enough, but not the truth. What she had confirmed up there was that she was now ready to learn the way through the forest; she had come of age, and was now capable of dying.

He was her guide, the young man who had come in out of the rain with a case of pneumonia. On the afternoon of the fifth day she went up to his room again. He was lying there getting well, weak and content, thinking about a morning ten years ago when he had walked out with his father and grandfather past the quarries, an April morning on a dry plain awash with sunlight and blue flowers. After they had passed the Chorin Company quarries they suddenly began to talk politics, and he understood that they had come out of town onto the empty plain in order to say things aloud, in order to let him hear what his father said: "There'll always be enough ants to fill up all the ant-hills—worker ants, army ants." And the grandfather, the dry, bitter, fitful man, in his seventies angrier and gentler than his son, vulnerable as his thir-teen-year-old grandson: "Get out, Kosta, why don't you get out?" That was only a taunt. None of them would run away, or get away. A man, he walked with men across a barren plain blue with flow-ers in brief April; they shared with him their anger, their barren helpless obduracy and the brief blue fire of their anger. Talking aloud under the open sky, they gave him the key to the house of manhood, the prison where they lived and he would live. But they had known other houses. He had not. Once his grandfather, Ste-fan Fabbre, put his hand on young Stefan's shoulder while he spoke. "What would we do with freedom if we had it, Kosta? What has the West done with it? Eaten it. Put it in its belly. A great wondrous belly, that's the West. With a wise head on top of it, a man's head, with a man's mind and eyes—but the rest all belly. He can't walk any more. He sits at table eating, eating, thinking up machines to bring him more food, more food. Throwing food to the black and yellow rats under the table so they won't gnaw down the walls around him. There he sits, and here we are, with nothing in our bellies but air, air and cancer, air and rage. We can still walk. So we're yoked. Yoked to the foreign plow. When we smell food we bray and kick. —Are we men, though, Kosta? I doubt it." All the time his hand lay on the boy's shoulder, tender, almost deferent, because the boy had never seen his inheritance at all but had been born in jail, where nothing is any good, no anger, understanding, or pride, nothing is any good except obduracy, except fidelity. Those remain, said the weight of the old man's hand on his shoulder. So when a blonde girl came into his room where he lay weak and content, he looked at her from that sun-washed barren April plain with trust and welcome, it being irrelevant to this moment that his grandfather had died in a deportation train and his father had been shot along with forty-two other men on the plain outside town in the reprisals of 1956. "How do you feel?" she said, and he said, "Fine."

"Can I bring you anything?"

He shook his head, the same black-and-white head she had seen clear and unintelligible as Greek words on a white page, but now his eyes were open and he spoke her language. It was the same voice that had called faintly from the black woods of fever, the neighborhood of death, a few nights ago, which now said, "I can't remember your name." He was very nice, he was a nice fellow, this Stefan Fabbre, embarrassed by lying there sick, glad to see her. "I'm Bruna, I come next after Kasi. Would you like some books? Are you getting bored yet?" — "Bored? No. You don't know how good it is to lie here doing nothing, I've never done that. Your parents are so kind, and this big house, and the fields outside there —I lie here thinking, Jesus, is this me? In all this peace, in all this space, in a room to myself doing nothing?" She laughed, by which he knew her: the one who had laughed in rain and darkness before lights broke over the hill. Her fair hair was parted in the middle and waved on each side down nearly to the light, thick eyebrows; her eyes were an indeterminate color, unclear, grey-brown or grey. He heard it now indoors in daylight, the tender and exultant laugh. "Oh you beauty, you fine proud filly-foal never broken to harness, you scared and restive, gentle girl laughing . . ."

Wanting to keep her he asked, "Have you always lived here?" and she said, "Yes, summers," glancing at him from her indeterminate, shining eyes in the shadow of fair hair. "Where did you grow up?"

"In Sfaroy Kampe, up north."

"Your family's still there?"

"My sister lives there." She still asked about families. She must be very innocent, more elusive and intact even than Kasimir, who placed his reality beyond the touch of any hands or asking of identity. Still to keep her with him, he said, "I lie here thinking. I've thought more already today than in the last three years."

"What do you think of?"

"Of the Hungarian nobleman, do you know that story? The one that was taken prisoner by the Turks, and sold as a slave. It was in the sixteenth century. Well, a Turk bought him, and yoked him to a plow, like an ox, and he plowed the fields, driven with a whip. His family finally managed to buy him back. And he went home, and got his sword, and went back to the battlefields. And there he took prisoner the Turk that had bought him, owned him. Took the Turk back to his manor. Took the chains off him, had him brought outside. And the poor Turk looked around for the impaling stake, you know, or the pitch they'd rub on him and set fire to, or the dogs, or at least the whip. But there was nothing. Only the Hungarian, the man he'd bought and sold. And the Hungarian said, 'Go on back home. . . .'"

"Did he go?"

"No, he stayed and turned Christian. But that's not why I think of it."

"Why do you?"

"I'd like to be a nobleman," Stefan Fabbre said, grinning. He was a tough, hard fellow, lying there nearly defeated but not defeated. He grinned, his eyes had a black flicker to them; at twenty-five he had no innocence, no confidence, no hope at all of profit. The lack of that was the black flicker, the coldness in his eyes. Yet he lay there taking what came, a small man but hard, possessing weight, a man of substance. The girl looked at his strong, blunt hands on the blanket and then up at the sunlit windows, thinking of his being a nobleman, thinking of the one fact she knew of him from Kasimir, who seldom mentioned facts: that he shared a tenement room in Krasnoy with five other students, three beds were all they could fit into it. The room, with three high windows, curtains pulled back, hummed with the silence of September afternoon in the country. A boy's voice rang out from fields far away. "Not much chance of it these days," she said in a dull soft voice, looking down, meaning nothing, for once wholly cast down, tired, without tenderness or exultation. He would get well, would go back a week late to the city, to the three bedsteads and five roommates, shoes on the floor and rust and hairs in the washbasin, classrooms, laboratories, after that employment as an inspector of sanitation on State farms in the north and northeast, a two-room flat in State housing on the outskirts of a town near the State foundries, a black-haired wife who taught the third grade from State-approved textbooks, one child, two legal abortions, and the hydrogen bomb. Oh was there no way out, no way? "Are you very clever?"

"I'm very good at my work."

"It's science, isn't it?"

"Biology. Research."

Then the laboratories would persist; the flat became perhaps a four-room flat in the Krasnoy suburbs; two children, no abortions, two-week vacations in summer in the mountains, then the hydrogen bomb. Or no hydrogen bomb. It made no difference.

"What do you do research on?"

"Certain molecules. The molecular structure of life."

That was strange, the structure of life. Of course he was talking down to her; things are not briefly described, her father had said, when one is talking of life. So he was good at finding out the molecular structure of life, this fellow whose wordless cry she had heard faintly from congested lungs, from the dark neighborhood and approaches of his death; he had called out and "Poor child," her mother had whispered, but it was she who had answered, had followed him. And now he brought her back to life.

"Ah," she said, still not lifting her head, "I don't understand all that. I'm stupid."

"Why did they name you Bruna, when you're blonde?"

She looked up startled, laughed. "I was bald till I was ten months old." She looked at him, seeing him again, and the future be damned, since all possible futures ever envisaged are — rusty sinks, two-week vacations and bombs or collective fraternity or harps and houris — endlessly, sordidly dreary, all delight being in the present and its past, all truth too, and all fidelity in the word, the flesh, the present moment: for the future, however you look at it, contains only one sure thing and that is death. But the moment is unpredictable. There is simply no telling what will happen. Kasimir came in with a bunch of red and blue flowers and said, "Mother wants to know if you'd like milk-toast for supper."

"Oatbread, oatbread," Bruna sang arranging the cornflowers and poppies in Stefan's water-glass. They ate oats three times a day here, some poultry, turnips, potatoes; the little brother Antony raised lettuce, the mother cooked, the daughters swept the big house; there was no wheat-flour, no beef, no milk, no housemaid, not any more, not since before Bruna was born. They camped here in their big old country house, they lived like gypsies, said the mother: a professor's daughter born in the middle class, nurtured and married in the middle class, giving up order, plenty, and leisure without complaint but not giving up the least scruple of the discriminations she had been privileged to learn. So Kasimir for all his gentleness could still hold himself untouched. So Bruna still thought of herself as coming next after Kasimir, and asked about one's family. So Stefan knew himself here in a fortress, in a family, at home. He and Kasimir and Bruna were laughing aloud together when the father came in. "Out," Dr Augeskar said, standing heroic and absolute in the doorway, the sun-king or a solar myth; his son and daughter, laughing and signalling child-like to Stefan behind his back, went out. "Enough is enough," Augeskar said, ausculting, and Stefan lay guilty, smiling, child-like.

The seventh day, when Stefan and Kasimir should have taken bus and train back to Krasnoy where the University was now open, was hot. Warm darkness followed, windows open, the whole house open to choruses of frogs by the river, choruses of crickets in the furrows, a southwest wind bearing odors of the forest over dry autumn hills. Between the curtains billowing and going slack burned six stars, so bright in the dry dark sky that they might set fire to the curtains. Bruna sat on the floor by Stefan's bed, Kasimir lay like a huge wheatstalk across the foot of it, Bendika, whose husband was in Krasnoy, nursed her five-month-old firstborn in a chair by the empty fireplace. Joachim Bret sat on the windowsill, his shirtsleeves rolled up so that the bluish figures OA46992 were visible on his lean arm, playing his guitar to accompany an English lute-song:

Yet be just and constant still, Love may beget a wonder,
Not unlike a summer's frost or winter's fatal thunder:
He that holds his sweetheart dear until his day of dying
Lives of all that ever lived most worthy the envying.

Then, since he liked to sing praise and blame of love in all the languages he knew and did not know, he began to strum out "Plaisir d'Amour," but came to grief on the shift of key, while the baby was sat up to belch loudly causing merriment. The baby was flung aloft by Kasimir while Bendika protested softly, "He's full, Kasi, he'll spill." — "I am your uncle. I am Uncle Kasimir, my pockets are full of peppermints and papal indulgences. Look at me, whelp! You don't dare vomit on your uncle. You don't dare. Go vomit on your aunt." The baby stared unwinking at Bruna and waved its hands; its fat, silky belly showed between shirt and diaper. The girl returned its gaze as silently, as steadily. "Who are you?" said the baby. "Who are you?" said the maiden, without words, in wonder, while Stefan watched and faint chords in A sobbed joyously on Bret's guitar between the lighted room and the dark dry night of autumn. The tall young mother carried the baby off to bed, Kasimir turned off the light. Now the autumn night was in the room, and their voices spoke among the choruses of crickets and frogs on the fields, by the streams. "It was clever of you to get sick, Stefan," said Kasimir, lying again across the foot of the bed, long arms white in the dusk. "Stay sick, and we can stay here all winter."

"All year. For years. Did you get your fiddle fixed?"

"Oh yes. Been practicing the Schubert. Pa, pa, poum *pah.*"

"When's the concert?"

"Sometime in October. Plenty of time. Poum, poum—swim, swim, little trout. Ah!" The long white arms sawed vaguely a viol of dusk. "Why did you choose the bass viol, Kasimir?" asked Bret's voice among frogs and crickets, across marshbottoms and furrows, from the windowsill. "Because he's shy," said Bruna's voice like a country wind. "Because he's an enemy of the feasible," said Stefan's dark dry voice. Silence. "Because I showed extraordinary promise as a student of the cello," said Kasimir's voice, "and so I was forced to consider, did I want to perform the Dvorak Concerto to cheering audiences and win a People's Artist award, or did I not? I chose to be a low buzz in the background. Poum, pa poum. And when I die, I want you to put my corpse in the fiddle case, and ship it rapid express deep-freeze to Pablo Casals with a label saying 'Corpse of Great Central European Cellist.' " The hot wind blew through the dark. Kasimir was done, Bruna and Stefan were ready to pass on, but Joachim Bret was not able to. He spoke of a man who had been helping people get across the border; here in the southwest rumors of him were thick now; a young man, Bret said, who had been jailed, had escaped, got to England, and come back; set up an escape route, got over a hundred people out in ten months, and only now had been spotted and was being hunted by the secret police. "Quixotic? Traitorous? Heroic?" Bret asked. "He's hiding in the attic now," Kasimir said, and Stefan added, "Sick of milk-toast." They evaded and would not judge; betrayal and fidelity were immediate to them, could not be weighed any more than a pound of flesh, their own flesh. Only Bret, who had been born outside prison, was excited, insistent. Prevne was crawling with agents, he went, even if you went to buy a newspaper your identification was checked. "Easier to have it tattooed on, like you," said Kasimir. "Move your foot, Stefan." — "Move your fat rump, then." — "Oh, mine are German numbers, out of date. A few more wars and I'll run out of skin." — "Shed it, then, like a snake." — "No, they go right down to the bone." — "Shed your bones, then," Stefan said, "be a jellyfish. Be an amoeba. When they pin me down, I bud off. Two little spineless Stefans where they thought they had one MR 64100282A. Four of them, eight, sixteen thirty-two sixty-four a hundred and twenty-eight. I would entirely cover the surface of the globe were it not for my natural enemies." The bed shook, Bruna laughed in darkness. "Play the English song again, Joachim," she said.

Yet be just and constant still, Love may beget a wonder . . .

"Stefan," she said in the afternoon light of the fourteenth day as she sat, and he lay with his head on her lap, on a green bank above the river-marshes south of the house. He opened his eyes: "Must we go?"

"No."

He closed his eyes again, saying, "Bruna." He sat up and sat beside her, staring at her. "Bruna, oh God! I wish you weren't a virgin." She laughed and watched him, wary, curious, defenseless. "If only—here, now—I've got to go away day after tomorrow!" — "But not right under the kitchen windows," she said tenderly. The house stood thirty yards from them. He collapsed by her burying his head in the angle of her arm, against her side, his lips on the very soft skin of her forearm. She stroked his hair and the nape of his neck.

"Can we get married? Do you want to get married?"

"Yes, I want to marry you, Stefan."

He lay still awhile longer, then sat up again, slowly this time, and looked across the reeds and choked, sunlit river to the hills and the mountains behind them.

"I'll have my degree next year."

"I'll have my teaching certificate in a year and a half."

They were silent awhile.

"I could quit school and work. We'll have to apply for a place . . ." The walls of the one rented room facing a courtyard strung with sooty washing rose up around them, indestructible. "All right," he said. "Only I hate to waste this." He looked from the sunlit water up to the mountains. The warm wind of evening blew past them. "All right. But Bruna, do you understand . . ." that all this is new to me, that I have never waked before at dawn in a high-windowed room and lain hearing the perfect silence, never walked out over fields in a bright October morning, never sat down at table with fair, laughing brothers and sisters, never spoken in early evening by a river with a girl who loved me, that I have known that order, peace, and tenderness must exist but never hoped even to witness them, let alone possess them? And day after tomorrow I must go back. No, she did not understand. She was only the country silence and the blessed dark, the bright stream, the wind, the hills, the cool house; all that was hers and her; she could not understand. But she took him in, the stranger in the rainy night, who would destroy her. She sat beside him and said softly, "I think it's worth it, Stefan, it's worthwhile."

"It is. We'll borrow. We'll beg, we'll steal, we'll filch. I'll be a great scientist, you know. I'll create life in a test-tube. After a squalid early career Fabbre rose to sudden prominence. We'll go to meetings in Vienna. In Paris. The hell with life in a test-tube! I'll do better than that, I'll get you pregnant within five minutes, oh you beauty, laugh, do you? I'll show you, you filly, you little trout, oh you darling—" There under the windows of the house and under the mountains still in sunlight, while the boys shouted playing tennis up beside the house, she lay soft, fair, heavy in his arms under his weight, absolutely pure, flesh and spirit one pure will: to let him come in, let him come in.

Not now, not here. His will was mixed, and obdurate. He rolled away and lay face up in the grass, a black flicker in his eyes looking at the sky. She sat with her hand on his hand. Peace had never left her. When he sat up she looked at him as she had looked at Bendika's baby, steadily, with pondering recognition. She had no praise for him, no reservation, no judgment. Here he is; this is he.

"It'll be meager, Bruna. Meager and unprofitable."

"I expect so," she said, watching him.

He stood up and brushed grass off his trousers. "I love Bruna!" he shouted, lifting his hand; and from the sunlit slopes across the river-marshes where dusk was rising came a vague short sound, not her name, not his voice. "You see?" he said standing over her, smiling. "Echoes, even. Get up, the sun's going, do you want me to get pneumonia again?" She reached out her hand, he took it and pulled her up to him. "I'll be very loyal, Bruna," he said. He was a small man and when they stood together she did not look up to him but straight at him at eyelevel. "That's what I have to give," he said, "that's all I have to give. You may get sick of it, you know." Her eyes, grey-brown or grey, unclear, watched him steadily. In silence he raised his hand to touch for a moment, with reserve and tenderness, her fair parted hair. They went back up to the house, past the tennis court where Kasimir on one side of the net and the two boys on the other swung, missed, leapt and shouted. Under the oaks Bret sat practicing a guitar-tune. "What language is that one?" Bruna asked, standing light in the shadow, utterly happy. Bret cocked his head to answer, his misshapen right hand lying across the strings. "Greek; I got it from a book; it means, 'O young lovers who pass beneath my window, can't you see it's raining?' " She laughed aloud, standing by Stefan who had turned to watch the three run and poise on the tennis court in rising shadow, the ball soar up from moment to moment into the level gold light.

He walked into Prevne next day to buy their tickets with Kasimir, who wanted to see the weekly market there; Kasimir took joy in markets, fairs, auctions, the noise of people getting and selling, the barrows of white and purple turnips, racks of old shoes, mounds of print cotton, stacks of bluecoated cheese, the smell of onions, fresh lavender, sweat, dust. The road that had been long the night they came was brief in the warm morning. "Still looking for that get-em-out-alive fellow, Bret says," said Kasimir. Tall, frail, calm, he moseyed along beside his friend, his bare head bright in the sunlight. "Bruna and I want to get married," Stefan said.

"You do?"

"Yes."

Kasimir hesitated a moment in his longlegged amble, went on, hands in his pockets. Slowly on his face appeared a smile. "Do you really?"

"Yes."

Kasimir stopped, took his right hand out of his pocket, shook

Stefan's. "Good work," he said, "well done." He was blushing a little. "Now that's something real," he said, going on, hands in his pockets; Stefan glanced at his long, quiet young face. "That's absolute," Kasimir said, "that's real." After a while he said, "That beats Schubert."

"Main problem is finding a place to live, of course, but if I can borrow something to get started on, Metor still wants me for that project—we'd like to do it straight off—if it's all right with your parents, of course." Kasimir listened fascinated to these chances and circumstances confirming the central fact, just as he watched fascinated the buyers and sellers, shoes and turnips, racks and carts of a market-fair that confirmed men's need of food and of communion. "It'll work out," he said. "You'll find a place." — "I expect so," said Stefan never doubting it. He picked up a rock, tossed it up and caught it, hurled it white through sunlight far into the furrows to their left. "If you knew how happy I am, Kasimir —" His friend answered, "I have some notion. Here, shake hands again." They stopped again to shake hands. "Move in with us, eh, Kasi?" — "All right, get me a truckle-bed." They were coming into town. A khaki-colored truck crawled down Prevne's main street between flyblown shops, old houses painted with garlands long faded; over the roofs rose high yellow hills. Under lindens the market square was dusty and sun-dappled: a few racks, a few stands and carts, a noseless man selling sugarcandy, three dogs cringingly, unwearingly following a white bitch, old women in black shawls, old men in black vests, the lanky keeper of the Post-Telephone Bar leaning in his doorway and spitting, two fat men dickering in a mumble over a pack of cigarettes. "Used to be more to it," Kasimir said. "When I was a kid here. Lots of cheese from Portacheyka, vegetables, mounds of 'em. Everybody turned out for it." They wandered between the stalls, content, aware of brotherhood. Stefan wanted to buy Bruna something, anything, a scarf; there were buttonless mud-colored overalls, cracked shoes. "Buy her a cabbage," Kasimir said, and Stefan bought a large red cabbage. They went into the Post-Telephone Bar to buy their tickets to Aisnar. "Two on the S.W. to Aisnar, Mr Praspayets." —

"Back to work, eh?" — "Right." Three men came up to the counter, two on Kasimir's side one on Stefan's. They handed over. "Fabbre Stefan, domicile 136 Tome Street, Krasnoy, student, MR 64100282A. Augeskar Kasimir, domicile 4 Sorden Street, Krasnoy, student, MR 80104944A. Business in Aisnar?" — "Catching the train to Krasnoy." The men returned to a table. "In here all day, past ten days," the innkeeper said in a thready mumble, "kills my business. I need another hundred kroner, Mr Kasimir; trying to short-change me?" Two of the men, one thickset, the other slim and wearing an army gunbelt under his jacket, were by them again. The smiling innkeeper went blank like a television set clicked off. He watched the agents go through the young men's pockets and feel up and down their bodies; when they had gone back to the table he handed Kasimir his change, silent. They went out in silence. Kasimir stopped and stood looking at the golden lindens, the golden light dappling dust where three dogs still trotted abased and eager after the white bitch, a fat housewife laughed with an old cackling man, two boys dodged yelling among the carts, a donkey hung his grey head and twitched one ear. "Oh well," Stefan said. Kasimir said nothing. "I've budded off," Stefan said, "come on, Kasi." They set off slowly. "Right," Kasimir said straightening up a little. "It's not relevant, you know," said Stefan. "Is the innkeeper really named Praspayets?" — "Evander Praspayets. Has a brother runs the winery here, Belisarius Praspayets." Stefan grinned, Kasimir smiled a little vaguely. They were at the edge of the market-place about to cross the street. "Damn, I forgot my cabbage in the bar," Stefan said, turning, and saw some men running across the market-place between the carts and stalls. There was a loud clapping noise. Kasimir grabbed at Stefan's shoulder for some reason, but missed, and stood there with his arms spread out, making a coughing, retching sound in his throat. His arms jerked wider and he fell down, backwards, and lay at Stefan's feet, his eyes open, his mouth open and full of blood. Stefan stood there. He looked around. He dropped on his knees by Kasimir who did not look at him. Then he was pulled up and held by the arm; there were men around him and one of them was waving something, a paper, saying loudly, "This is him, the traitor, this is what happens to traitors. These are his forged papers. This is him." Stefan wanted to get to Kasimir, but was held back; he saw men's backs, a dog, a woman's red staring face in the background under golden trees. He thought they were helping him to stand, for his knees had given under him, but as they forced him to turn and walk he tried to pull free, crying out, "Kasimir!"

He was lying on his face on a bed, which was not the bed in the high-windowed room in the Augeskar house. He knew it was not but kept thinking it was, hearing the boys calling down on the tennis court. Then understanding that it was his room in Krasnoy and his roommates were asleep he lay still for a long time, despite a fierce headache. Finally he sat up and looked around at the pine-plank walls, the grating in the door, the stone floor with cigarette butts and dried urine on it. The guard who brought his breakfast was the thickset agent from the Post-Telephone Bar, and did not speak. There were pine splinters in the quicks of his nails on both his hands; he spent a long time getting them out.

On the third day a different guard came, a fat dark-jowled fellow reeking of sweat and onions like the market under the lindens. "What town am I in?" — "Prevne." The guard locked the door, offered a cigarette through the grating, held a lighted match through. "Is my friend dead? Why did they shoot him?" — "Man they wanted got away," said the guard. "Need anything in there? You'll be out tomorrow." — "Did they kill him?" The guard grunted yes and went off. After a while a half-full pack of cigarettes and a box of matches dropped in through the grating near Stefan's feet where he sat on the cot. He was released next day, seeing no one but the dark-jowled guard who led him to the door of the village lock-up. He stood on the main street of Prevne half a block down from the market-place. Sunset was over, it was cold, the sky clear and dark above the lindens, the roofs, the hills.

His ticket to Aisnar was still in his pocket. He walked slowly and carefully to the market-place and across it under dark trees to the Post-Telephone Bar. No bus was waiting. He had no idea when they ran. He went in and sat down, hunched over, shaking with cold, at one of the three tables. Presently the owner came out from a back room.

"When's the next bus?" He could not think of the man's name, Praspets, Prayespets, something like that. "Aisnar, eight-twenty in the morning," the man said. — "To Portacheyka?" Stefan asked after a pause. — "Local to Portacheyka at ten." — "Tonight?" — "Ten tonight." — "Can you change this for a . . . ticket to Portacheyka?" He held out his ticket for Aisnar. The man took it and after a moment said, "Wait, I'll see." He went off again to the back. Stefan got change ready for a cup of coffee, and sat hunched over. It was seven-ten by the white-faced alarm clock on the bar. At seven-thirty when three big townsmen came in for a beer he moved as far back as he could, by the pool table, and sat there facing the wall, only glancing round quickly now and then to check the time on the alarm clock. He was still shaking, and so cold that after a while he put his head down on his arms and shut his eyes. Bruna said, "Stefan."

She had sat down at the table with him. Her hair looked pale as cotton round her face. His head still hunched forward, his arms on the table, he looked at her and then looked down.

"Mr Praspayets telephoned us. Where were you going?"

He did not answer.

"Did they tell you to get out of town?"

He shook his head.

"They just let you go? Come on. I brought your coat, here, you must be cold. Come on home." She rose, and at this he sat up; he took his coat from her and said, "No. I can't."

"Why not?"

"Dangerous for you. Can't face it, anyway."

"Can't face us? Come on. I want to get out of here. We're driving back to Krasnoy tomorrow, we were waiting for you. Come on, Stefan." He got up and followed her out. It was night now. They set off across the street and up the country road, Bruna holding a flashlight beamed before them. She took his arm; they walked in silence. Around them were dark fields, stars.

"Do you know what they did with . . ."

"They took him off in the truck, we were told."

"I don't— When everybody in the town knew who he was—" He felt her shrug. They kept walking. The road was long again as when he and Kasimir had walked it the first time without light. They came to the hill where the lights had appeared, the laughter and calling all round them in the rain. "Come faster, Stefan," the girl beside him said timidly, "you're cold." He had to stop soon, and breaking away from her went blind to the roadside seeking anything, a fencepost or tree, anything to lean against till he could stop crying; but there was nothing. He stood there in the darkness and she stood near him. At last he turned and they went on together. Rocks and weeds showed white in the ragged circle of light from her flashlight. As they crossed the hillcrest she said with the same timidity and stubbornness, "I told mother we want to marry. When we heard they had you in jail here I told her. Not father, yet. This was—this was what he couldn't stand, he can't take it. But mother's all right, and so I told her. I'd like to be married quite soon, if you would, Stefan." He walked beside her, silent. "Right," he said finally. "No good letting go, is there." The lights of the house below them were yellow through the trees; above them stars and a few thin clouds drifted through the sky. "No good at all."

1962

An die Musik

"A PERSON ASKING TO SEE YOU, SIR. Mr. Gaye."

Otto Egorin nodded. This being his only free afternoon in Foranoy, it was inevitable that some young hopeful would find him out and waste it. He knew from the way his man said "person" that it was no one important. Still, he had been buried so long in managing his wife's concert tour that it was refreshing to receive a postulant of his own. "Show him in," he said, turning again to the letter he was writing, and did not look up till the visitor was well into the room and had had time to be impressed by the large, bald head of Otto Egorin engrossed in writing a letter. That first impression, Otto knew, would keep all but the brashest ones down. This one did not look brash: a short, shabby man leading a small boy by the hand and stammering about the great liberty —valuable time—great privilege—"Well, well," said the impresario, moderately genial, since if not put at ease the timid often wasted more time than the brash, "playing chords since he could sit up, and the Appassionata since he was three? Or do you write your own sonatas, eh, my man?" The child stared at him with cold dark eyes. The man stammered and halted, "I'm very sorry, Mr. Egorin, I wouldn't have—my wife's not well, I take the boy out Sunday afternoons, so she doesn't have to look after him—" It was really painful to see him going red, then pale, then red. "He'll be no trouble," he blundered on.

"What is it about then, Mr. Gaye?" asked Otto rather dryly.

"I write music," Gaye said, and Otto saw then what he had missed in supposing the child to be yet another prodigy: the small roll of music-paper under the visitor's arm.

"All right, good. Let me see it, please," he said, putting out his hand. This was the point he dreaded with the shy ones. But Gaye did not explain for twenty minutes what he had tried to do and why and how, all the time clutching his compositions and sweating. He gave the roll of music to Egorin without a word, and at Egorin's gesture sat down on the stiff hotel sofa, the little boy beside him, both of them nervous, submissive, with their strange, steady, dark eyes. "You see, Mr. Gaye, this is all that matters, after all, eh? This music you bring me. You bring it to me to look at: I want to look at it: so, please excuse me while I do so." It was his usual speech after he had pried the manuscript away from a shy-talkative one. This one merely nodded. "It's four songs and p-part of a Mass," he said in his barely audible voice.

Otto frowned. He had been saying lately that he had had no idea how many idiots wrote songs until he married a singer. The first he glanced at relieved his suspicions, being a duet for tenor and baritone, and he remembered to smoothe the frown off his forehead. The last of the four caught his attention, a setting of a Goethe lyric. He moved very slightly as he sat at the desk, a mere twitch towards the piano, instantly repressed. No use raising hopes; to play a note of their stuff was to convince them at once that they were Beethoven and would be produced in the capital by Otto Egorin within the month. But it was a real bit of writing, that tune with the clever, yearning, quiet little accompaniment. He went on to the Mass, or rather three fragments of a Mass, a Kyrie, Benedictus, and Sanctus. The writing was neat, rapid, and crowded; music-paper is not cheap, thought Otto, glancing at his visitor's shoes. At the same time he was hearing a solo tenor voice over a queer racket from organ, trombones, and double-basses, "Benedictus qui venit in nomine Domini"—very queer stuff; but no, there now, just when it's about to drive you mad it all turns to crystal, so simply, so simply you'd swear it was crystal all along. And the tenor, the poor devil singing double-piano way up there, find me the tenor who can do that and fight off the trombones too. The Sanctus: now, splendid, the trumpet, really splendid—Otto looked up. He had been tapping the side of his hand on the desk, nodding, grinning, muttering. That had blown it. "Come here!" he said angrily. "What's your name? What's this?"

"Ladislas Gaye. The—the— That's the second trumpet."

"Why isn't it marked? Here, take it, play it!"

They went through the Sanctus five times. "Planh, pla-anh, planh!" Otto blared, a trumpet. "All right! Why do your basses come in there, one-two-three-four-*boom* in come the basses like elephants, where does that get you?"

"Back to the Sanctus, listen, here's the organ under the tenors," and the piano roared under Gaye's husky tenor, "Sabaoth, then the cellos and the elephants, four, *Sanctus! Sanctus! Sanctus!*"

He sat back from the piano, Otto took his eyes from the score. The room was silent.

Otto set straight a drooping red rose in the bouquet on the top of the hired piano. "And where do you expect to have this Mass sung?"

The composer was silent.

"Women's chorus. Double men's chorus. Full orchestra; brass choir; organ. Well, well. Let me see those songs again. Is this all you've written of the Mass?"

"The Credo isn't orchestrated yet."

"I suppose you'll throw in double tympani for that? All right, here, where is it, the Goethe. Let me play." He played through the song twice, then sat twiddling out one of the queer half-spoken phrases of the accompaniment. "It's first rate, you know," he said. "Absolutely first rate. What the devil. Are you a pianist? What are you?"

"A clerk."

"A clerk? What kind of clerk? This is your hobby, eh, your amusement in spare time?"

"No, this is . . . this is what I . . ."

Otto looked up at the man: short and shabby, white with excitement, inarticulate.

"I want to know something about you, Gaye! You barge in, 'I write music,' you show me a little music, very good. Very good, this song, the Sanctus, the Benedictus too, that's real work, I want to read it again. But I've been shown good writing before. Have you been performed? How old are you?"

"Thirty."

"What else have you written?"

"Nothing else of any size—"

"At thirty? Four songs and half a Mass?"

"I haven't much time to work."

"This is nonsense. Nonsense! You don't write this kind of thing without practice. Where did you study?"

"Here, at the Schola Cantorum—till I was nineteen."

"With whom? Berdicke, Chey?"

"Chey and Mme Veserin."

"Never heard of her. And this is all you'll show me?"

"The rest isn't good, or isn't finished—"

"How old were you when you wrote this song?"

Gaye hesitated. "Twenty, I think."

"Ten years ago! What have you been doing since? You 'want to write music,' eh? Well, write it! What else can I say? This is good, absolutely good, and so is that racket with the trombones. You can write music, but, my dear man, what can I do about it? Can I produce four songs and half a Mass by an unknown student of Vaslas Chey? No. You want encouragement, I know. Well, that I give. I encourage you. I encourage you to write more music. Why don't you?"

"I realise this is very little," Gaye brought out stiffly. His face was contorted, one hand was fiddling and pulling at the knot of his tie. Otto was sorry for him and unnerved by him. "Very little, why not make it more?" he said, genial. Gaye looked down at the piano keys, put his hand on them; he was shaking. "You see," he began, then turned away with a jerk, stooping, hiding his face with his hands, and broke into sobs. Otto sat like a stone on the piano bench. The small boy, forgotten all this time, sitting with his grey-stockinged legs hanging over the edge of the sofa, slipped down and ran to his father; of course he was blubbering too, but he kept pulling at his father's coat, trying to get at his hand, whispering, "Papa, don't, papa, please don't." Gaye knelt and put his arm around the child. "Sorry, Vasli, don't worry, it's all right. . . ." But he was not yet in control of himself. Otto rose with some majesty, and called in his wife's maid. "Take the laddie, go give him candy, make him happy, eh?" The girl, a calm Swiss who knew all Central Europeans were mad, nodded, ignoring the weeping man, and said, "Come, what's your name?"

The child held on to his father.

"Go with her, Vasli," Gaye said. The child let her take his hand, and went out with her.

"You have a fine little boy," said Otto. "Now, sit down, Gaye. Brandy? A little, eh?" He opened and shut desk drawers, puffed and grunted to himself, put a glass in Gaye's hand, sat down again at the desk.

"I can't—" Gaye began, worn out, at rock bottom.

"No, you can't; neither can I; these things happen. You were more surprised than I, perhaps. But listen now, Ladislas Gaye. I have no time for the woes of all the world, I have a great many cares of my own and I'm very busy. But since we've come so far, I'd like to know what makes you break down like this."

Gaye shook his head. With the submissiveness that had vanished only while they were going through his score, he answered Otto's questions. He had had to quit the music school when his father died; he now supported his mother, his wife, his three children on his pay as clerk for a plant that made ballbearings and other small steel parts. He had worked there eleven years. Four evenings a week he gave piano lessons, for which they let him use a practice-room at the Schola Cantorum.

Otto did not find much to say for a while. "The good Lord has seen fit to give you bad luck," he remarked. Gaye did not reply. Indeed, good or bad luck seemed hardly adequate to describe this kind of solid, persevering mismanagement of the world, from which Ladislas Gaye and most other men suffered, and Otto Egorin, for no clear reason, did not. "Why did you come to see me, Gaye?"

"I had to. I knew what you'd have to say, that I haven't written enough. But when I heard you were to be here, I swore to myself I'd see you, I had to. They know me at the Schola, but they're busy with their students, of course; since Chey died there's no one who ... I had to see you. Not for encouragement, but to see a man who lives for music, who arranges half the concerts in the country, who stands for . . . for . . ."

"For success," said Otto Egorin. "Yes, I know. I wanted to be a composer. When I was twenty, in Vienna, I used to go look at the house where Mozart lived, I used to go stare at Beethoven's tomb in the cemetery. I called on Mahler, on Richard Strauss, every composer who came to Vienna. I soaked myself in their success, the dead and the living. They had written music and it was played. Even then, you see, I knew I was not a real composer, and I needed their reality, to make life mean anything at all. That's not your problem. You need only to be reminded that there is music—eh? That not everyone makes steel ballbearings."

Gaye nodded.

"Is there no one else," Otto asked abruptly, "to take care of mama?"

"My sister married a Czech fellow, they live in Prague. . . . And she's bedridden, my mother."

"Yes. And there would still be the wife with the nervous disorder, and the kids, eh, and the bills, and the steel-ballbearings plant. . . . Well, Gaye, I don't know. You know, there was Schubert. I often wonder about Schubert, it's not just you that makes me think of him. Why did God create Franz Schubert? To expiate some other men's sins? Also, why did he kill the man off the moment he reached the level of the last quintet? —But Schubert didn't wonder why God had created him. To write music, of course. *Du holde Kunst, ich danke dir!* Incredible. The little, sickly, ugly crackpot with glasses, scribbling his music like any other crackpot, never hearing it played—*Du holde Kunst!* How would you say it, 'thou gracious Art, thou kindly Art'? As if any art were kindly, gracious, gentle! Have you ever thought of throwing it over, Gaye? Not the music. The rest."

He met the gaze of the strange, cold, dark eyes and refused to be ashamed, to apologise. Gaye had said that he, Otto Egorin, lived for music. He did. He might be a good bourgeois; he might be very sorry for a poor devil who needed nothing in God's world but a little cash in order to be a good composer; but he would not apologise to the poor devil's sick mother and sick wife and three brats. If you live for music you live for music.

"I'm not made so."

"Then you're not made to write music."

"You thought differently when you were reading my Sanctus."

"Du lieber Herr Gott!" Otto exploded. He was a great patriot, but his mother and his upbringing had been Viennese and in moments of real emotion he reverted to German. "All right! Did it ever occur to you, my dear young man, that you incur a certain responsibility in writing something like that Sanctus? That you become answerable? That music has no arthritis, no nervous disorders, no hungry potbelly and 'Papa, papa, I want this, I want that,' but all the same she depends on you, on you alone? Other men can feed brats and keep sick women. But no other man can write your music!"

"Yes, I know that."

"But you're not quite sure anyone would undertake to feed the brats and keep the women. Probably they wouldn't. Doch, doch —you're too gentle, too gentle, Gaye." Otto strode up and down the room on his bandy legs, snorting and grimacing.

"When I finish the Mass may I send it to you?"

"Yes. Yes, of course. I shall be pleased to see it. When will it be? Ten years from now? 'Gaye, who the devil's Gaye, where did I meet him—this is good—a young fellow, he shows promise—' And you'll be forty, getting tired, ready for a little arthritis or nervous disorder yourself. Certainly send me your Mass! . . . You have great talent, Gaye, you have great courage, but you're too gentle, you must not try to write a big work like this Mass. You can't serve two masters. Write songs, short pieces, something you can think of while you work at this Godforsaken steel plant and write down at night when the rest of the family's out of the way for five minutes. Write them on anything, unpaid bills, whatever, and send them to me, don't think you have to pay two and a half kroner a sheet for this fine paper, you can't afford fine paper—when they're printed is time to think of that. Send me songs, not ten years from now but a month from now, and if they're as good as this Goethe song I'll give you a section on my wife's program in Krasnoy in December. Write little songs, not impossible Masses. Hugo Wolf, you know—Hugo Wolf wrote only songs, eh?"

He thought that Gaye, overcome with gratitude, was going to break down again, and though apprehensive he felt pleased with himself, wise, generous: he had made the poor fellow happy and might get something from him, too. The accompaniment to the Goethe song was still running in his head, spare, dry, sorrowful, beautiful. Then Gaye began to speak and Otto realised, slowly, but without real surprise, that it was not gratitude at all. "The Mass is what I've got to write, what I have in me. The songs come, sometimes a lot of them together, but I've never been able to write them at will, it has to be a good day. But the Mass, and a symphony I've been working on, they have size and weight, you see, they carry themselves along over the weeks, and I can always work on them when I have time. I know the Mass is ambitious. But I know all I want to say in it. It will be good. I've learned how to do what I must do, you see. I've begun it, I have to finish it."

Otto had stopped in his pacing back and forth and was watching him with an expression both of incredulity and longsuffering familiarity. "Bah!" he said. "What the devil do you come to me for? And burst into tears? And then tell me thanks very much for your suggestion but I shall continue to attempt the impossible? The arrogance, the unreasonableness—no, I can endure all that—but the stupidity, the absolute stupidity of artists, I cannot stand it any longer!"

Abashed, submissive, Gaye sat there in his shabby suit; everything about him was shabby, pinched, overstrained and underfed, ground down and worn thin; and Otto knew he could shout at him for two hours and promise him introductions, publication, performances. He would never be heard. Gaye would only say in his inaudible stammer, "I have to write the Mass first. . . ."

"You read German, eh?"

"Yes."

"All right. After the mass is finished, then write songs. In German. Or French if you like it, people are used to it, they won't listen in Vienna or Paris to a lot of songs in a language like ours, or Rumanian or Danish or what have you, it's a mere curiosity, like folksongs. We want your music heard, so write for the big countries, and remember most singers are idiots. All right?"

"You're very kind, Mr. Egorin," Gaye said, not submissively this time but with a curious formal dignity. He knew that Otto was yielding to his stubborn unreason as he would to that of a great, a famous artist, humoring him, getting round him, when he could as well have stepped on him like a beetle. He knew, in fact, that Otto was defeated.

"If you'll put the elephants aside for a very little while, for a few evenings, in order to write something which might conceivably be published, be heard, you see," Otto was saying, still ironic, exasperated, and deferent, when the door swung open and his wife made an entrance. She swept Gaye's little son in with her, the Swiss maid followed. The room all at once was full of men, women, children, voices, perfume, jewelry. "Otto, look what I found with Anne Elise! Did you ever see such an enchanter? Look at the eyes, the great, dark, solemn eyes! 'His name is Vasli, he likes chocolates.' Such an enchanter, such a little man, did you ever see such a child? How do you do, so glad. You're Vasli's—? yes, of course, you are, the eyes! Oh, Christ, what a ghastly hole this town is, I want to leave on the first train after the concert, Otto, I don't care if it's three in the morning. I can feel myself beginning to look like all those huge empty stone houses across the river, all eyes, staring, staring, staring, like skulls! Why don't they tear them down if nobody lives in them? Never again, never again, to hell with the provinces and encouraging national art, I can't sing in every graveyard in the country, Otto. Anne Elise, draw my bath, please. I'm simply filthy, I must be grey as buckwheat. Are you the Management from Sorg?"

"I've already talked to them on the telephone," said Otto, knowing that Gaye would be unable to answer. "Mr Gaye is a composer, he writes Masses." He did not say "songs," for that would catch Egorina's attention. He was paying Gaye back a little, giving him an object lesson in practicality. Egorina, uninterested in Masses, talked on. An unceasing flood of words poured from her for twenty-four hours before each concert, and stopped only when she walked out on the stage, tall, magnificent, smiling, to sing. After she had sung she would be quiet, ruminating. She was, Otto said, the most beautiful musical instrument in the world. He had married her because it was the only way to keep her from going on the light-opera stage; stubborn, stupid, and sensitive in proportion to her talent, she dreaded failure and wanted to suc-ceed the sure way. So Otto had married her and made her succeed the hard way, as a lieder-singer. In October she would take her first opera role, Strauss's *Arabella.* That probably meant she would talk for six straight weeks beforehand. Otto could bear it. She was very beautiful, and generally good-humored, and anyway one need not listen. She did not care whether one listened so long as one was there, an audience.

She talked on, the sound of rushing water came from the bath-room, the telephone rang, she began to talk on the telephone. Gaye had not said a word. The child stood beside him, grave as ever; Egorina had forgotten all about Vasli after making her entrance with him, and had been swearing like a sergeant.

Gaye stood up. Relieved, Otto took him to the door, gave him two passes to Egorina's recital tomorrow night, shrugged off his thanks—"We're not sold out, you know! This is a dead town for music." Behind them Egorina's voice flooded magnificently on, her laugh broke out like the jet of a great fountain. "Jesus! what do I care what that little Jew says?" she sang out, and again the great, golden laugh. "Gaye," said Otto Egorin, "you know, there's one other thing. This is not a good world for music, either. This world now, in 1938. You're not the only man who wonders, what's the good? who needs music, who wants it? Who indeed, when Europe is crawling with armies like a corpse with maggots, when Russia uses symphonies to glorify the latest boiler-factory in the Urals, when the function of music has been all summed up in Putzi playing the piano to soothe the Leader's nerves. By the time your Mass is finished, you know, all the churches may be blown into little pieces, and your men's chorus will be wearing uniforms and also being blown into little pieces. If not, send it to me, I shall be interested. But I'm not hopeful. I am on the losing side, with you. So is she, my Egorina there, believe it or not. She will never believe it. . . . But music is no good, no use, Gaye. Not any more. Write your songs, write your Mass, it does no harm. I shall go on arranging concerts, it does no harm. But it won't save us. . . ."

Ladislas Gaye and his son walked from the hotel to the old bridge over the Ras; their home was in the Old City, the bleak jumbled quarter on the north side of the river. What Foranoy had in the way of wealth and modernity lay south of the river in the New City. It was a warm bright day, late spring; they stopped on the bridge to look at the arches reflecting in the dark water, each with its reflection forming a perfect circle. A barge came through loaded with wadded crates and Vasli, held up by his father so he could see over the stone railing, spat down on one of the crates. "Shame on you," Ladislas Gaye said without heat. He was happy. He did not care if he had blubbered like a baby in front of Otto Egorin, the great impresario. He did not care if he was tired and this was one of his wife's bad days and he was already late. He did not care about anything at all, except the child's small, firm hand in his, and the way the wind out here on the bridge, between city and city, carried away all sound and left one bathed in warm, silent sunlight, and the fact that Otto Egorin knew what he was: a musician. So far, in this one recognition by one man, he was strong and he was free. It went no further than that, his strength and freedom, but it was enough. The trumpet-tune of his Sanctus sang in his head.

"Papa, why did the big lady have things in her ears and ask if I liked chocolate? Do people not like chocolate?"

"They were jewels, Vasli. I don't know." The trumpet sang on. If only he and the little fellow could stay here awhile, in the sunlight and silence, between city and city, between moment and moment . . . They went on, into the Old City, past the wharves, past the abandoned houses built of stone, up the hill, into the courtyard of their tenement. Vasli broke loose, disappeared into a crowd of children brawling, screaming, swarming in the court. Ladislas Gaye called after him, gave it up, climbed the dark stairs and went down a dark hall on the third floor, let himself in the dark kitchen, the first room of their three-room flat. His wife was peeling potatoes at the kitchen table. She wore a dirty white wrapper, dirty pink chenille mules on her bare feet. "It's six o'clock, Ladis," she said without looking round at him.

"I was in the New City."

"Why'd you drag the child so far? Where is he? Where are Tonia and Givana? I called and called them, I'm sure they're not in the court. Why'd you go so far with the child?"

"I went to—"

"My back aches worse than ever, it's the heat, why is summer so hot here?"

"Let me do that."

"No, I'll finish. I wish you'd clean those gas vents in the oven, Ladis, I must have asked you fifty times. Now I can't get it lighted at all, it's filthy dirty, and I can't go scraping at it with my back like it is."

"All right. Let me change my shirt."

"Listen here, Ladis—Ladis! Is Vasli down there in the court in his good clothes? Go down and get him right away, how do you think we can afford to get his good clothes cleaned every time he puts them on? Ladis? Go down and get him! Can you never think of these things? He's probably filthy dirty already, playing with those big roughnecks around the well!"

"I'm going, give me time, will you!"

In September the east wind of autumn rose, blowing past the empty stone houses and down the bright troubled river, blowing scant litter about the city streets, blowing fine dust into people's eyes and throats as they went home from work. Ladislas Gaye passed a street-orator, a little girl crying loudly as she ran down the steep street, a newspaper kiosk where the headlines said "Mr Neville Chamberlain in Munich," a big stalled automobile around which a crowd had gathered, a group of young fellows watching a fistfight, a couple of women talking earnestly to each other across the street, one standing on the curb and the other hanging half out of a tenement window, wearing a blue-and-scarlet satin wrapper; he saw and heard it all, and saw and heard nothing. He was very tired. He got home. His young daughters were playing in the court, in the well of shadow four stories deep. He saw them in the swarm of girls shrilling around an areaway, but did not stop. He went up the dark stairs, down the hall, into the kitchen. His wife had been stronger lately, as the weather began to cool, but now she was in a vile temper and ready to weep; little Vasli had been caught with older boys torturing a cat, pouring kerosene over it, they planned to set it afire. "He's no good, he's a little beast, how could a child want to do a horrible thing like that?" Vasli was locked in the middle room, screaming with rage. Ladislas Gaye sat down at the kitchen table and put his head in his hands. He felt sick. His wife went on about the child, the other children in the court. "That Mrs Rasse, sticking her head in here without even knocking and saying did I know what my little Vasli was up to, as if her brats were something to be proud of, with their dirty faces and pink eyes like a lot of rabbits. Are you going to do anything about it, Ladis, are you just going to sit there? Do you think I can handle him? Is that the kind of son you want?"

"What can I do about it? Are we going to have anything to eat tonight? I've got a piano lesson at eight, you know. For God's sake let me sit down a minute, let me have some peace."

"Peace! You want peace, what do you care if the child turns into a brute like all the others here! All right, what do I care either if that's what you want." She slapped about the kitchen in her pink mules, getting supper.

"Little children are cruel," he said. "They don't know what it means. They find out."

She shrugged. Vasli was sobbing now behind the door; he knew his father was home. Presently Ladislas Gaye went into that room, sat with the child in the half-dark. In the third room, where the grandmother lay in bed, dance music blared from the radio; Ladislas had bought it secondhand for her, it was her sole amusement and she never talked now of anything but what she heard on the radio. Vasli clung to his father, not crying any more, worn out. "You mustn't do anything like that with the other boys, Vasli," the father murmured at last. "The poor beast is weaker than you, it can't help itself."

The child was silent. All cruelty, all misery, all darkness present and to come hung around them in the dark room. Trombones blared a waltz in the next room. He clung to his father, silent.

In the thick blaring of the trombones, thick as sweet cough-sirup, Gaye heard for a moment the deep clear thunder of his Sanctus like thunder between the stars, over the edge of the universe—one moment of it, as if the roof of the building had been taken off and he looked up into the complete, enduring darkness, one moment only. The announcer talked, a smooth excited gabble. When Gaye went back to the kitchen he said to his wife, over the shrill voices of the two girls, "The English Prime Minister is in Munich with Hitler." She did not answer, only set the food down in front of him, soup and potatoes. She was still overwrought and angry. "Eat and don't talk, you, shameless!" she snapped at Vasli, who had forgotten it all and was squabbling with his sisters.

As Gaye walked down the hill, across the bridge over the Ras in late dusk, a tune he had written was in his head. It was the last of seven poems he had set, all in a burst, in August; he kept wondering if that was enough to copy out and send to Otto Egorin in Krasnoy. But the last verse of the poem bothered him now, the one that meant, "It is Thou in thy mercy that breakest down over our heads all we build, that we may see the sky: and so I do not complain." He had muffed that last line; it should go thus—Gaye sang it to himself, sang the whole verse over, heard the accompaniment. There it was, that was it. Pray God his pupil would be late so that he could work it out on the piano at the Schola before the lesson. But it was he who was late. When the lesson was over his head was full of Clementi exercises and though the melody was set now he could not get the accompaniment clear; as he had heard it on the bridge it had been purer, more certain. He tried the verse, the whole song, over and over, but the janitor was through cleaning and wanted to close the building. He started home. The wind was strong and cold now, the sky empty, the river black as oil under the arches of the bridge. He stopped there on the bridge a while, but could not hear the music he had heard.

Back at home he sat down at the kitchen table with the manuscript of the song, but with the weaker version before his eyes and no piano at hand he lost even the mood of the accompaniment he wanted; it was all out of reach. He knew he was too tired to work but nonetheless tried, doggedly, angrily, to hear and to write down. He sat half an hour motionless, never moving his hand. At the other end of the table his wife was mending Tonia's dress, listening to some program of talk on the grandmother's radio. He put his hands over his ears. She said something about music, but he did not listen. The total impossibility of writing was a choking weight in him, like a big chunk of rock in his chest. Nothing would ever change, he thought, and in the next moment he felt a relaxation within him, lightness, openness, and certainty, utter certainty. He thought it was his own song, then, raising his head, understood that he was actually hearing this tune. He did not have to write it. It had been written long ago, no one need suffer for it any more. Lehmann was singing it,

Du holde Kunst, ich danke dir.

He sat still a long time. Music will not save us, Otto Egorin had said. Not you, or me, or her, the big golden-voiced woman who had no children and wanted none; not Lehmann who sang the song; not Schubert who had written it and was a hundred years dead. What good is music? None, Gaye thought, and that is the point. To the world and its states and armies and factories and Leaders, music says, "You are irrelevant"; and, arrogant and gentle as a god, to the suffering man it says only, "Listen." For being saved is not the point. Music saves nothing. Merciful, uncaring, it denies and breaks down all the shelters, the houses men build for themselves, that they may see the sky.

Gaye put away the scribbled, ruled sheets of paper, the little volume of poetry, the pen and ink. He stretched and yawned. "Good night," he said in his soft voice, and went off to bed.

1938

The House

THE SUNLIGHT of any October lay yellow across her way, and hundreds of dry, golden afternoons rustled under her steps. Only their great age kept the sycamores from being importunate. For blocks she was pursued by the familiarity of shadows, bricks, and balconies. Fountains spoke to her as if she had not been away at all. Eight years she had been gone, and this stupid city had never noticed her absence; its sunlight and the sound of its many waters hung about her like the walls of her own house, her home. Confused and offended, she passed the house at 18 Reyn Street without a glance at its door or garden wall, though something, not her eyes, saw that door and gate were locked. After that, the city began to let her be. Within a block or two it did not know her. The fountains talked to someone else. Now she was differently confused, recognising none of these crossings, not one doorstep or window of the shops and houses. She had to ask her way ignominiously of street-signs and house-numbers, and when she found the place she sought, a tenement with several entrances, she had to enter and inquire at open doors. Rumpled beds, family quarrels and partly buttoned dressing-gowns sent her up to a fourth-floor room, where her knock was answered only by a pencilled card tacked on the door. F.L. PANIN, it said. She looked in. A dormer room, jammed with the hefty sofas and tables of a dismantled house; a stranger's room, sunny, stuffy, defenseless.

Across from her was a curtained doorway. She said, "Anybody here?" and was answered from behind the curtain by someone half awake, "Hold on a moment."

She held on.

He came across the room, himself, as wholly himself as the stones and sunlight of the city after these eight years: the reality of her wretched dreams in which he and she stopped at inns on roads leading up into grey mountains and could not find, down cold corridors, each other's room: the original of all the facsimiles who, in Krasnoy on winter evenings, crossed a street with his walk or looked round with his turn of the head: himself.

"Sorry, I was asleep."

"I'm Mariya."

He stood still, and his coat hung on him as on a coatrack. Seeing that, she saw that his hair had gone a kind of dull grey—that his hair was grey. He was thin, grey, changed. She would not have known him if she passed him on the street. They shook hands.

"Sit down, Mariya," he said, and they both sat, in large shabby chairs. Across the bare floor between them lay a bar of Aisnar's unalloyed, inimitable autumn sunlight. "I have the alcove, but the Panins let me use this room while they're out. They both work the day shift at the GPR."

"That's where you work too—evening shift? I was going to leave a note."

"Usually I'd be on the way to work by this time. I've had some days off. Flu."

She should have expected him not to ask any questions. He disliked answering them, and seldom asked them. It was his self-respect that prevented him, a self-respect so entire that it included all other men and women, accepted them as responsible, exempted them from question. How had he survived so long in this world of the public confessional?

"I have a two-week holiday," she said. "I work in Krasnoy, teaching. In the primary schools."

It confused her to see his smile on the face of a man she did not know.

"I'm divorced from Givan."

He looked down at the sunlight on the floor. She answered the next question he did not ask—"Four years ago." Then she took out her cigarettes in self-defense. But she summoned up courage, before laying the smokescreen, to offer him one, reaching out to him across the sunlight: "Smoke?"

"Yes, thanks." He looked at the cigarette, smelled it, and leaned forward happily to the flame of her match. He inhaled the smoke and burst into a cough, a hacking, whacking cough, a series of explosions like heavy artillery, the most noise she had ever heard him make in his life. All through it he held on to the cigarette, and when he had got his breath back he took another draw, not inhaling.

"You shouldn't smoke," she said helplessly.

"Haven't been," he said. Sweat stood out on his forehead, even in his hair, which she now saw was only partly grey. Soon he put the cigarette out with care and stowed the unsmoked end in his shirt pocket. This he did with grace and ease, but then he looked at her with apology. She had not been with him during the years when he learned to save cigarette butts, and so might be embarrassed; and she tried to look impassive, knowing how he disliked causing embarrassment.

The strangers' room, the furniture of some other house, stood silently around them.

"Mariya, what did you come here for?" The question, which would have been any other man's, was not his, nor the voice; only the eyes, clear, frank, and obdurate.

"To see you. To talk to you, I mean, Pier. It got so that I had to. I'm lonely. I mean, more than that, I'm alone. By myself. Outside. There's nobody in Krasnoy that I can say anything to, they don't need me. I used to think, while we were married, you know, that if I were by myself, on my own, I'd find a lot of interesting people, friends, and be on the inside, do you know what I mean? But that was all wrong. You had friends then and I expect you do now. You have a place to stand on when you meet people. I never did, I never made friends. I never have reached another person, except you. I suppose I didn't really want to reach anybody. But now I do." She stopped, and with the same horror with which she had heard him cough, heard herself sob loudly. "I can't stand it very much longer. Everything is falling apart. I've lost my nerve." She went on as fast as she could. "Are people here buying salt? You can't get salt any more in Krasnoy, people buy it all and save it, they say if you wrap yourself in a sheet soaked in salt water it will cure radiation burns. Is that true? I don't know. Is everyone here scared? But it's not just the bombs, there are the other things they talk about, germ warfare, and how there are too many people and more all the time, so soon we'll all be like rats in a box. And nobody seems to really hope for anything good any more. And then you get older, and you think about dying, and in a time like this it seems so mean and pointless. Living and dying both. It's like being alone at night in the wind, it just blows right through me. I try to hold myself up and have some dignity, you know, but I can't believe in it any more, I feel like an ant in a swarm, I can't do it alone!"

To spare her or himself he had gone to stand at the window, and with his back still turned he spoke, gently. "Nobody can," he said. "But you can't turn back, my dear. Nobody can do that either."

"I'm not trying to turn back. Truly I'm not. I'm just trying to meet you, now, here, don't you see? Here where we are now. Because you're the only person I ever have met. All the others are on different roads, they live in other houses. Didn't you ever think I'd have to come back to you?"

"I never once thought it."

"But I never left you, Pier! I only ran away because I knew I belonged to you, and I thought the only way I'd ever be myself was to get free of you. Myself, myself, a lot of good myself was. All I did was run like a stupid bitch till I got to the end of my leash."

"Well, leashes have two ends," he said, leaning forward as if to gaze through the glass at a rooftop, a cloud, a remote grey mountain-peak. "I let go."

She tried to smooth her hair, which escaped in fierce tendrils from the knotted braids, red-blonde. Her voice was still shaky, but she said with dignity, "I wasn't talking about love, Pier."

"Then I don't understand."

"I meant loyalty. Taking somebody in as part of your own life. Either you do or you don't. We did. I was disloyal. You let me go, but you aren't capable of disloyalty."

He came back to the chair facing her and sat down. Now she had the courage to look at him, and made sure that his face had not in fact changed; it had been eroded, erased, by sickness or hard times: not change, only loss.

"Look, my dear"—that word was most comfortable to Mariya, though she knew it was only the expression of his general kindliness—"look, my dear, no matter how you put it, you're trying to go back. There's nothing left to go back to. In any sense." And he looked at her with that kindness, as if he wished he could soften the facts.

"What happened? Will you tell me? Not now if you don't want. Sometime. I talked to Moshe, but I didn't want to ask questions about you. I came here thinking you still lived in the house in Reyn Street and . . . all the rest."

"Well, during the Pentor Government we published some works that got the House into trouble when the R.E.P. came back into force. Bernoy, if you remember him, Bernoy and I were tried that fall. We were in prison up north. They let me out two years ago. But of course I can't work for the state now in a responsible position, and that cuts out working for the House." He still called it "the House," the publishing firm Korre and Sons, which his family had owned and run from 1813 to 1946. When the firm was nationalised he had been kept on as manager. That had been his position when Mariya met him and married him and when she left him, and she had never imagined the chance of his losing it.

He took the cigarette end out of his shirt pocket, took up a matchbox from a table, then hesitated. "Well, what it amounts to is that where I am now isn't where I was during our marriage. I'm nowhere in particular, you see. And we're well out of it. Loyalty really isn't relevant, at this point." He lit the cigarette and very cautiously got a mouthful of smoke.

The table-lamp had a purple, ball-fringed shade to it, something left over from another world. Mariya fiddled with this, tugging at the dusty purple balls as if counting them around the shade. Her face was knotted in a frown. "Well, but where does loyalty count except in a tight place? You sound as if you'd given up, Pier!"

Silence gave assent.

"I haven't been in trouble or in jail, and I have a job, and a room to myself. I'm much better off. But look at me. Like a lost dog. You can at least respect yourself, no matter what they've taken from you, but what I've lost is just that—self-respect."

"You," he said, suddenly white with anger, "you took away my self-respect eight years ago!"

This was not true, but she did not blame him for believing it. She persisted: "All right, then neither of us has any, there's nothing to prevent our meeting."

Silence gave no assent.

Mariya counted off nine cotton balls, then another nine. "What I mean, I ought to say it, Pier, is that I want to see if we can meet again; if I can come to you. Not come back, just come. I could be some help to you, as things are. I was just coming begging, but I didn't know. . . . I can get transferred to a school here. At least we might find a couple of rooms, and when you're ill it's a help to have somebody to look after things. It would be a better arrangement than this, for both of us. It would be more sensible." Her face began to contract with tears again. She could not keep from crying, and got up to go. Her sleeve caught in the ball-fringed shade and pulled the lamp down with a smash. "Oh I'm sorry I came! I'm sorry!" she cried, picking up the lamp, struggling to refit the shade. He took it from her. "The bulb broke, see, the shade clamps onto the bulb. Don't cry, Mariya. We'll have to get a new bulb for it. Please, my dear. It's all right."

"I'll go get the new bulb. Then I'll go."

"I didn't say go." He moved back from her. "I didn't say come, either. I don't know what to say. You go off with that bastard Givan Pelle, divorce me, and then come back to tell me loyalty's the only thing that counts. Does it? Did mine? You told me then that fidelity is a bourgeois pretense invented by married people who haven't the courage to live free."

"I didn't say that, I repeated it, couldn't you tell I learned it from Givan!"

"I don't care where you learned it, you said it, to me!" He gasped for breath. He looked down at the lampshade askew over the socket, and after a minute said, "All right. Wait." He sat down, and neither spoke. A golden beam slid imperceptibly up through the air of the room as the sun's end of it slid down towards the quiet plowlands west of Aisnar. She saw his face through a dust of gold. He had been a handsome man, when they married, fourteen years ago. A handsome, happy man, proud and kind, very good at his work. There had been a splendor to him, a wholeness.

That was gone. There was no more room in the world for whole people, they took up too much space. What she had done to him was only a part of the general program for cutting him and people like him down to size, for chopping and paring and breaking up, so that in the texture of life nothing large, nothing hard, nothing grand should remain.

A gilt-framed mirror hung over the clothes-chest, and she went to it to repair her braids. It reflected the brown air of a parlour long ago dispersed, the walls torn down: but in the mirror the blinds were still drawn. Her face was there only as a blur among many silvery plaques of blindness. She looked behind the curtain and saw a kerosene stove, a cot, a couple of packing-boxes serving as pantry and bureau. She looked at the cot and thought of the oaken bedstead in the house in Reyn Street, white sheets open and the white coverlet thrown back, on hot mornings of summer waking to the sound of fountains through windows left open to moonlight and now radiant with sunlight, the white curtains blowing a little; summers of marriage.

"Ouf," she sighed, squeezed so flat between past and present that she could not breathe. "There should be some place to go, some direction to things, shouldn't there. . . . Pier, what happened to Bernoy?"

"Typhus. In jail."

"I remember him with that girl, the one who dropped her pearls in the wine, but they were imitation pearls."

"Nina Farbey."

"Did they ever marry?"

"No, he married the eldest Akoste girl. She lives over on the east side now, I see her now and then. They had two boys." He stood up, rubbing his face, and now came past her to get a necktie and comb from the box by his bed. He made himself neat, peering into the mirror that refused to see him.

"Listen, Pier, I want to tell you something. A while after we married, Givan told me that one reason he'd wanted to marry me was he knew I couldn't have children. I don't know, he said a lot of things like that, they didn't mean much. But it made me think, it made me see that perhaps that's really what made me leave you. When I found out I couldn't have children, after the miscarriage, you know, it didn't seem so bad. But I kept on feeling lighter and lighter, as if there was nothing to me, I didn't weigh anything, and it didn't matter what I did. But you were real, what you did still mattered. Only I didn't matter at all."

"I wish you'd told me that."

"I didn't know it then."

"Come, let's go on."

"I'll go; it's cold. Is there a shop near?"

"I want to get out." They went down the rattling stairs. At the first breath outside he gasped like a diver into a mountain lake and fired off a short volley of his coughs, but then went on all right. They walked fast because it was cold and because the cold and the golden light and blocks of blue shadow exhilarated them. "How is so-and-so," she asked of various old acquaintances, and he told her. He had not slipped out of the net of friendship, acquaintance, alliance by blood, marriage, work, or temperament, woven over a hundred and thirty years by his family and their House, secured by his status in a provincial city, and enlarged by his own sociable character. She had thought of herself as one born for few, passionate friendships, out of place at the polite and cheerful dinner-tables and firesides of his life. Now she thought she had not been

153

out of place, only envious. She had begrudged him to his friends, she had envied the gifts he gave them: his courtesy, his kindness, his affection. She had envied him his competence and pleasure in the act of living.

They went into a hardware shop and he asked for a forty-watt light bulb. While the man was finding it and filling out the Government sales forms for it, Mariya got the money ready. Pier had already put money on the counter.

"I broke it," she said in an undertone.

"You're a visitor. It's my lamp."

"No it's not, it's the Panins'."

"Here you are," he said gracefully, and the man took his money. Cheered by this victory, he asked as they left the shop, "Did you come by Reyn Street?"

"Yes."

He smiled; his face was vivid, the low sun shining full on it. "Did you look at the house?"

"No."

"I knew you hadn't!" The reddish light kindled him like a match. "Come along, let's go look at it. It hasn't changed at all. Would you like to?—if you don't, please say so. I couldn't go past it, when I first got back." They were now walking back together the way she had come alone. "That, of course," he went on quite light-heartedly, "is my reef, my undoing. Yours is isolation. Mine's owning. Love of place. Love of one place. People are not really important to me, you know, as they are to you. But after a while I saw the trick, the point, just as you did; it's the same thing, loyalty. I mean, ownership and loyalty don't actually depend on each other. You lose the place, but you keep the loyalty. Now I like to go by the house. They used it for a Government office for a while, printing forms or something, I'm not sure what it's used for now."

They were soon walking on the dry leaves of sycamores between the walls of gardens and the calm, ornate fronts of old houses. The wind of the autumn evening smelled very sweet. They stopped and looked at the house at 18 Reyn Street: a gold stucco front; an iron balcony over the door that opened straight onto the street; a high, beautiful window to either side of the door, and three windows above. A crab-apple tree leaned over the wall of the garden. In spring the windows of the east bedrooms opened on the froth and spume of its flowering. In the square before the house a fountain played in a shallow basin, and standing near the gate in the wall they heard the small babbling reply of the little naiad-fountain in the garden. When the windows were open in summer the murmur of water filled the house. Against the locked door, the locked gate, the drawn blinds, she remembered open windows filled with moonlight, sunlight, leaves, the sound of water and of voices.

"Property is theft," Pier Korre said dreamily, looking at his house.

"It looks empty. All the blinds are drawn."

"Yes, it does. Well, come along."

After a block or two she said, "Nothing leads anywhere. We come and stand in the street like tourists. Your family built it, you were born in it, we lived in it. Years and years. Not just our years, all the years. All broken off. It's all in pieces."

While they walked, separated sometimes by a hurrying man or an old woman pushing a barrow-load of firewood, as the narrow streets of Aisnar filled up with people coming from work, she kept talking to him. "It's not just human isolation, loneliness, that I can't stand any more. It's that nothing holds together, everything is broken off, broken up—people, years, events. All in pieces, fragments, not linked together. Nothing weighs anything any more. You start from nothing, and so it doesn't matter which way you go. But it *must* matter."

Avoiding a pushcart of onions, he said either, "It should," or, "It doesn't."

"It does. It must. That's why I'm back here. We had a way to go, isn't that true? That's what marriage is, it means making a journey together, night and day. I was afraid of going ahead, I thought I'd get lost, my precious self, you know. So I ran off. But I couldn't, there was nowhere else to go. There's only one way. At twenty-one I married you and here it is fourteen years and two divorces later and I'm still your wife. I always was. Everything I ever did since I was twenty has been done for you, or to you, or with you, or against you. Nobody else counted except in comparison, or relation, or opposition to you. You're the house to which I come home. Whether the doors are open or locked."

He walked along beside her, silent.

"Can I stay here, Pier?"

His voice hardly freed itself from the jumble of voices and noises in the street: "There are no doors. No house left."

His face was tired and angry; he did not look at her. They reached his tenement and climbed the stairs and came into the Panins' flat.

"We could find something better than this," she said with timidity. "Some privacy . . ."

The room was dusky, the window a square of void evening sky, without color. He sat down on the sofa. She put the new bulb in the socket, fixed the ball-fringed shade on it, switched it on and off again. Pier's body as he sat awkwardly relaxed, stripped of all grace and of the substance that holds a man down heavy on the earth, was like a shadow among the shadows. She sat down on the floor beside him. After a while she took his hand. They sat in silence; and the silence between them was heavy, was present, it had a long past, and a future, it was like a long road walked at evening.

People came heavy-footed into the room, switching on the lamp, speaking, staring: an ugly, innocent-looking couple in their twenties, he lank, she pregnant. Mariya jumped up smoothing her braids. Pier got up. "The Panins, Mariya," he said. "Martin, Anna, this is Mariya Korre. My wife."

1965

The Lady of Moge

THEY MET ONCE when they were both nineteen, and again when they were twenty-three. That they met only once after that, and long after, was Andre's fault. It was not the kind of fault one would have expected of him, seeing him at nineteen years old, a boy poised above his destiny like a hawk. One saw the eyes, the hawk-eyes, clear, unblinking, fierce. Only when they were closed in sleep did anyone ever see his face, beautiful and passive, the face of the hero. For heroes do not make history—that is the historians' job—but, passive, let themselves be borne along, swept up to the crest of the tide of change, of chance, of war.

She was Isabella Oriana Mogeskar, daughter of the Counts of Helle and the Princes of Moge. She was a princess, and lived in a castle on a hill above the Molsen River. Young Andre Kalinskar was coming to seek her hand in marriage. The Kalinskar family coach rolled for half an hour through the domains of Moge, came through a walled town and up a steep fortified hill, passed under a gateway six feet thick, and stopped before the castle. The high wall was made splendid by an infinite tracery of red vines, for it was autumn; the chestnut trees of the forecourt were flawless gold. Over the golden trees, over the towers, stood the faint, clear, windy sky of late October. Andre looked about him with interest. He did not blink.

In the windowless ground-floor hall of the castle, among saddles and muskets and hunting, riding, fighting gear the two old companions-at-arms, Andre's father and Prince Mogeskar, embraced. Upstairs where windows looked out to the river and the rooms were furnished with the comforts of peace, the Princess Isabella greeted them. Reddish-fair, with a long, calm, comely face and grey-blue eyes—Autumn as a young girl—she was tall, taller than Andre. When he straightened from his bow to her he straightened farther than usual, but the difference remained at least an inch.

They were eighteen at table that night, guests, dependents, and the Mogeskars: Isabella, her father, and her two brothers. George, a cheerful fifteen-year-old, talked hunting with Andre; the older brother and heir, Brant, glanced at him a couple of times, listened to him once, and then turned his fair head away, satisfied: his sister would not stoop to this Kalinskar fellow. Andre set his teeth, and, in order not to look at Brant, looked at his mother, who was talking with the Princess Isabella. He saw them both glance at him, as if they had been speaking of him. In his mother's eyes he saw, as usual, pride and irony, in the girl's—what? Not scorn; not approval. She simply saw him. She saw him clearly. It was exhilarating. He felt for the first time that esteem might be a motive quite as powerful as desire.

Late the next afternoon, leaving his father and his host to fight old battles, he went up to the roof of the castle and stood near the round tower to look out over the Molsen and the hills in the dying, windy, golden light. She came to him through the wind, across the stone. She spoke without greeting, as to a friend. "I've been wanting to talk with you."

Her beauty, like the golden weather, cheered his heart, made him both bold and calm. "And I with you, princess!"

"I think you're a generous man," she said. There was a pleasant husky tone, almost guttural, in her light voice. He bowed a little, and compliments pranced through his mind, but something prompted him to say only, "Why?"

"It's quite plain to see," she replied, impatient. "May I speak to you as one man to another?"

"As one man—?"

"Dom Andre, when I first met you yesterday, I thought, 'I have met a friend at last.' Was I right?"

Did she plead, or challenge? He was moved. He said, "You were right."

"Then may I ask you, my friend, not to try to marry me? I don't intend to marry."

There was a long silence.

"I shall do as you wish, princess."

"And without arguing!" cried the girl, all at once alight, aflame. "Oh, I knew you were a friend! Please, Dom Andre, don't feel sad or foolish. I refused the others without even thinking about it. With you, I had to think. You see, if I refuse to marry, my father will send me to the convent. So I can't refuse to marry, I can only refuse each suitor. You see?" He did; though if she had given him time to think, he would have thought that she must in the end accept either marriage or the convent, being, after all, a girl. But she did not give him time to think. "So the suitors keep coming; and it's like Princess Ranya, in the tale, you know, with her three questions, and all the young men's heads stuck on poles around the palace. It is so cruel and wearisome. . . ." She sighed, and leaning on the parapet beside Andre looked out over the golden world, smiling, inexplicable, comradely.

"I wish you'd ask me the three questions," he said, wistful.

"I have no questions. I have nothing to ask."

"Nothing to ask that I could give you, to be sure."

"Ah, you've already given me what I asked of you—not to ask me!"

He nodded. He would not seek her reasons; his rebuffed pride, and a sense of her vulnerability, forbade it. And so in her sweet perversity she gave them to him. "What I want, Dom Andre, is to be left alone. To live my life, my own life. At least till I've found out . . . The one thing I have questions to ask of, is myself. To live my own life, to find out my own way, am I too weak to do that? I was born in this castle, my people have been lords here for a long time, one gets used to it. Look at the walls, you can see why Moge has been attacked but never taken. Ah, one's life could be so splendid, God knows what might happen! Isn't it true, Dom Andre? One mustn't choose too soon. If I marry I know what will happen, what I'll do, what I'll be. And I don't want to know. I want nothing, except my freedom."

"I think," Andre said with a sense of discovery, "most women marry to get their freedom."

"Then they want less than I do. There's something inside me, in my heart, a brightness and a heaviness, how can I describe it? Something that exists and does not yet exist, which is mine to carry, and not mine to give up to any man."

Did she speak, Andre wondered, of her virginity or of her destiny? She was very strange, but it was a princely and a touching strangeness. In all she said, however arrogant and naïve, she was most estimable; and though desire was forbidden, she had reached straight into him to his tenderness, the first woman who had ever done so. She stood there quite alone, within him, as she stood beside him and alone.

"Does your brother know your mind?"

"Brant? No. My father is gentle; Brant is not. When my father dies, Brant will force me to marry."

"Then you have no one . . ."

"I have you," she said smiling. "Which means that I have to send you away. But a friend is a friend, near or far."

"Near or far, call to me if you need a friend, princess. I will come." He spoke with a sudden dignity of passion, vowing to her, as a man when very young will vow himself entirely to the rarest and most imperilled thing he has beheld. She looked at him, shaken from her gentle, careless pride, and he took her hand, having earned the right. Beyond them the river ran red under the sunset. "I will," she said. "I was never grateful to a man before, Dom Andre."

He left her, full of exaltation; but when he got to his room he sat down, feeling suddenly very tired, and blinking often, as if on the point of tears.

That was their first meeting, in the wind and golden light on the top of the world, at nineteen. The Kalinskars went back home. Four years passed, in the second of which, 1640, began the civil struggle for succession known as the War of the Three Kings.

Like most petty noble families the Kalinskars sided with Duke Givan Sovenskar in his claim to the throne. Andre took arms in his troops; by 1643, when they were fighting town by town down through the Molsen Province to Krasnoy, Andre was a field-captain. To him, while Sovenskar pushed on to the capital to be crowned, was entrusted the siege of the last stronghold of the Loyalists east of the river, the town and castle of Moge. So on a June day Andre lay, chin on folded arms, on the rough grass of a hilltop, gazing across a valley at the slate roofs of the town, the walls rising from a surf of chestnut leaves, the round tower, the shining river beyond.

"Captain, where do you want the culverins placed?"

The old prince was dead, and Brant Mogeskar had been killed in March, in the east. Had King Gulhelm sent troops across the river to the defense of his defenders, his rival might not be riding now to Krasnoy to be crowned; but no help had come, and the Mogeskars were besieged now in their own castle. Surrender they would not. Andre's lieutenant, who had arrived some days before him with the light troops, had requested a parley with George Mogeskar; but he had not even seen the prince. He had been received by the princess, he said, a handsome girl, but hard as iron. She had refused to parley: "Mogeskar does not bargain. If you lay siege we shall hold the castle. If you follow the Pretender we shall wait here for the King."

Andre lay gazing at the tawny walls. "Well, Soten, the problem's this: do we take the town first, or the castle?"

But that was not the problem at all. The problem was much crueller than that.

Lieutenant Soten sat down by him and puffed out his round cheeks. "Castle," he said. "Lose weeks taking that town, and then still have the castle to breach."

"Breach that—with the guns we've got? Once we're in the town, they'll accept terms in the castle."

"Captain, that woman in there isn't going to accept any terms."

"How do you know?"

"I've seen her!"

"So have I," said Andre. "We'll set the culverins there, at the south wall of the town. We'll begin bombardment tomorrow at dawn. We were asked to take the fort as it stands. It'll have to be at the cost of the town. They give us no choice." He spoke grimly, but was in his heart elated. He would give her every chance: the chance to withdraw from the hopeless fight and the chance, also, to prove herself, to use the courage she had felt heavy and shining in her breast, like a sword lying secret in its sheath.

He had been a worthy suitor, a man of her own mettle, and had been rejected. Fair enough. She did not want a lover, but an enemy; and he would be a worthy, an estimable one. He wondered if she yet knew his name, if someone had said, "Field-captain Kalinskar is leading them," and she had replied in her lordly, gentle, unheeding way, "Andre Kalinskar?"—frowning perhaps to learn that he had joined the Duke against the King, and yet not displeased, not sorry to have him as her foe.

They took the town, at the cost of three weeks and many lives. Later when Kalinskar was Marshal of the Royal Army he would say when drunk, "I can take any town. I took Moge." The walls were ingeniously fortified, the castle arsenal seemed inexhaustible, and the defenders fought with terrible spirit and patience. They withstood shelling and assaults, put out fires barehanded, ate air, in the last extremity fought face to face, house after house, from the town gate up to the castle scarp; and when taken prisoner they said, "It's her."

He had not seen her yet. He had feared to see her in the thick of that carnage in the narrow, ruined streets. From them at evening he kept looking up to the battlements a hundred feet above, the smoking cannon-emplacements, the round tower tawny red in sunset, the untouched castle.

"Wonder how we could get a match into the powder-store," said Lieutenant Soten, puffing his cheeks out cheerfully. His captain turned on him, his hawk-eyes red and swollen with smoke and weariness: "I'm taking Moge as it stands! Blow up the best fort in the country, would you, because you're tired of fighting? By God I'll teach you respect, Lieutenant!" Respect for what, or whom? Soten wondered, but held his tongue. As far as he was concerned, Kalinskar was the finest officer in the army, and he was quite content to follow him, into madness, or wherever. They were all mad with the fighting, with fatigue, with the glaring, grilling heat and dust of summer.

They bombarded and made assaults at all hours, to keep the defenders from rest. In the dark of early morning Andre was leading a troop up to a partial breach they had made by mining the outer wall, when a foray from the castle met them. They fought with swords there in the darkness under the wall. It was a confused and ineffectual scrap, and Andre was calling his men together to retreat when he became aware that he had dropped his sword. He groped for it. For some reason his hands would not grasp, but slid stupidly among clods and rocks. Something cold and grainy pressed against his face: the earth. He opened his eyes very wide, and saw darkness.

Two cows grazed in the inner courtyard, the last of the great herds of Moge. At five in the morning a cup of milk was brought to the princess in her room, as usual, and a little while later the captain of the fort came as usual to give her the night's news. The news was the same as ever and Isabella paid little heed. She was calculating when King Gulhelm's forces might arrive, if her messenger had got to him. It could not be sooner than ten days. Ten days was a long time. It was only three days now since the town had fallen, and that seemed quite remote, an event from last year, from history. However, they could hold out ten days, even two weeks, if they had to. Surely the King would send them help.

"They'll send a messenger to ask about him," Breye was saying.

"Him?" She turned her heavy look on the captain.

"The field-captain."

"What field-captain?"

"I was telling you, princess. The foray took him prisoner this morning."

"A prisoner? Bring him here at once!"

"He's got a sabre-cut on the head, princess."

"Can he speak? I'll go to him. What's his name?"

"Kalinskar."

She followed Breye through gilt bedrooms where muskets were stacked on the beds, down a long parqueted corridor that crunched underfoot with crystal from the shattered candle-sconces, to the ballroom on the east side, now a hospital. Oaken bedsteads, pillared and canopied, their curtains open and awry, stood about on the sweep of floor like stray ships in a harbor after storm. The prisoner was asleep. She sat down by him and looked at his face, a dark face, serene, passive. Something within her grieved; not her will, which was resolute; but she was tired, mortally tired and grieved, as she sat looking at her enemy. He moved a little and opened his eyes. She recognised him then.

After a long time she said, "Dom Andre."

He smiled a little, and said something inaudible.

"The surgeon says your wound is not serious. Have you been leading the siege?"

"Yes," he said, quite clearly.

"From the start?"

"Yes."

She looked up at the shuttered windows which let in only a dim hint of the hot July sunlight.

"You're our first prisoner. What news of the country?"

"Givan Sovenskar was crowned in Krasnoy on the first. Gulhelm is still in Aisnar."

"You don't bring good news, captain," she said softly, with indifference. She glanced round the other beds down the great room, and motioned Breye to stand back. It irked her that they could not speak alone. But she found nothing to say.

"Are you alone here, princess?"

He had asked her a question like that the other time, up on the rooftop in the sunset.

"Brant is dead," she answered.

"I know. But the younger brother . . . I hunted with him in the marshes, that time."

"George is here now. He was at the defense of Kastre. A mortar blew up. It blinded him. Did you lead the siege at Kastre, too?"

"No. I fought there."

She met his eyes, only for a moment.

"I'm sorry for this," she said. "For George. For myself. For you, who swore to be my friend."

"Are you? I'm not. I've done what I could. I've served your glory. You know that even my own soldiers sing songs about you, about the Lady of Moge, like an archangel on the castle walls. In Krasnoy they talk about you, they sing the songs. Now they can say that you took me prisoner, too. They talk of you with wonder. Your enemies rejoice in you. You've won your freedom. You have been yourself." He spoke quickly, but when he stopped and shut his eyes a moment to rest, his face looked still again, youthful. Isabella sat for a minute saying nothing, then suddenly got up and went out of the room with the hurrying, awkward gait of a girl in distress, graceless in her heavy, powder-stained dress.

Andre found that she was gone, replaced by the old captain of the fort, who stood looking down at him with hatred and curiosity.

"I admire her as much as you do!" he said to Breye. "More, more even than you here in the castle. More than anyone. For four years—" But Breye too was gone. "Get me some water to drink!" he said furiously, and then lay silent, staring at the ceiling. A roar and shudder—what was it?—then three dull thuds, deep and shocking like the pain in the root of a tooth; then another roar, shaking the bed—he understood finally that this was the bombardment, heard from inside. Soten was carrying out orders. "Stop it," he said, as the hideous racket went on and on. "Stop it. I need to sleep. Stop it, Soten! Cease firing!"

When he woke free of delirium it was night. A person was sitting near the head of his bed. Between him and the chair a candle burned; beyond the yellow globe of light about the candle-flame he could see a man's hand and sleeve. "Who's there?" he asked uneasily. The man rose and showed him in the full light of the candle a face destroyed. Nothing was left of the features but mouth and chin. These were delicate, the mouth and chin of a boy of about nineteen. The rest was newly healed scar.

"I'm George Mogeskar. Can you understand me?"

"Yes," Andre replied from a constricted throat.

"Can you sit up to write? I can hold the paper for you."

"What should I write?"

They both spoke very low.

"I wish to surrender my castle," Mogeskar said. "But I wish my sister to be gone, out of here, to go free. After that I shall give up the fort to you. Do you agree?"

"I—wait—"

"Write your lieutenant. Tell him that I will surrender on this one condition. I know Sovenskar wants this fort. Tell him that if she is detained, I shall blow the fort, and you, and myself, and her, into dust. You see, I have nothing much to lose, myself." The boy's voice was level, but a little husky. He spoke slowly and with absolute definiteness.

"The . . . the condition is just," Andre said.

Mogeskar brought an inkwell into the light, felt for its top, dipped the pen, gave pen and paper to Andre, who had managed to get himself half sitting up. When the pen had been scratching on the paper for a minute, Mogeskar said, "I remember you, Kalinskar. We went hunting in the long marsh. You were a good shot."

Andre glanced at him. He kept expecting the boy to lift off that unspeakable mask and show his face. "When will the princess leave? Shall my lieutenant give her escort across the river?"

"Tomorrow night at eleven. Four men of ours will go with her. One will come back to warrant her escape. It seems the grace of God that you led this siege, Kalinskar. I remember you, I trust you." His voice was like hers, light and arrogant, with that same husky note. "You can trust your lieutenant, I hope, to keep this secret."

Andre rubbed his head, which ached; the words he had written jiggled and writhed on the paper. "Secret? You wish this—these terms to be kept—you want her escape to be made secretly?"

"Do you think I wish it said that I sold her courage to buy my safety? Do you think she'd go if she knew what I am giving for her freedom? She thinks she's going to beg aid from King Gulhelm, while I hold out here!"

"Prince, she will never forgive—"

"It's not her forgiveness I want, but her life. She's the last of us. If she stays here, she'll see to it that when you finally take the castle she is killed. I am trading Moge Castle, and her trust in me, against her life."

"I'm sorry, prince," Andre said; his voice quavered with tears. "I didn't understand. My head's not very clear." He dipped the pen in the inkwell the blind man held, wrote another sentence, then blew on the paper, folded it, put it in the prince's hand.

"May I see her before she goes?"

"I don't think she'll come to you, Kalinskar. She is afraid of you. She doesn't know that it's I who will betray her." Mogeskar put out his hand into his unbroken darkness; Andre took it. He watched the tall, lean, boyish figure go hesitatingly off into the dark. The candle burned on at the bedside, the only light in the high, long room. Andre lay staring at the golden, pulsing sphere of light around the flame.

Two days later Moge Castle was surrendered to its besiegers, while its lady, unknowing and hopefull, rode on across the neutral lands westward to Aisnar.

And they met the third and last time, only by chance. Andre had not availed himself of Prince George Mogeskar's invitation to stop at the castle on his way to the border war in '47. To avoid the site of his first notable victory, to refuse a proud and grateful ex-enemy, was unlike him, suggesting either fear or a bad conscience, in neither of which did he much indulge himself. Nonetheless, he did not go to Moge. It was thirty-seven years later, at a winter ball in Count Alexis Helleskar's house in Krasnoy, that somebody took his arm and said, "Princess, let me present Marshall Kalinskar. The Princess Isabella Proyedskar."

He made his usual deep bow, straightened up, and straightened up still more, for the woman was taller than he by an inch at least.

Her grey hair was piled into the complex rings and puffs of the current fashion. The panels of her gown were embroidered with arabesques of seedpearls. Out of a broad, pale face her blue-grey eyes looked straight at him, an inexplicable, comradely gaze. She was smiling. "I know Dom Andre," she said.

"Princess," he muttered, appalled.

She had got heavy; she was a big woman now, imposing, firmly planted. As for him, he was skin and bone, and lame in the right leg.

"My youngest daughter, Oriana." The girl of seventeen or eighteen curtsied, looking curiously at the hero, the man who in three wars, in thirty years of fighting, had forced a broken country back into one piece, and earned himself a simple and unquestionable fame. What a skinny little old man, said the girl's eyes.

"Your brother, princess—"

"George died many years ago, Dom Andre. My cousin Enrike is lord of Moge now. But tell me, are you married? I know of you only what all the world knows. It's been so long, Dom Andre, twice this child's age. . . ." Her voice was maternal, plaintive. The arrogance, the lightness were gone, even the huskiness of passion and of fear. She did not fear him now. She did not fear anything. Married, a mother, a grandmother, her day over, a sheath with the sword drawn, a castle taken, no man's enemy.

"I married, princess. My wife died in childbirth, while I was in the field. Many years ago." He spoke harshly.

She replied, banal, plaintive, "Ah, but how sad life is, Dom Andre!"

"You wouldn't have said that on the walls of Moge," he said, still more harshly, for it galled his heart to see her like this. She looked at him with her blue-grey eyes, impassive, simply seeing him.

"No," she said, "that's true. And if I had been allowed to die on the walls of Moge, I should have died believing that life held great terror and great joy."

"It does, princess!" said Andre Kalinskar, lifting his dark face to her, a man unabated and unfulfilled. She only smiled and said in her level, maternal voice, "For you, perhaps."

Other guests came up and she spoke to them, smiling. Andre stood aside, looking ill and glum, thinking how right he had been never to go back to Moge. He had been able to believe himself an honest man. He had remembered, faithfully, joyfully, for forty years, the red vines of October, the hot blue evenings of midsummer in the siege. And now he knew that he had betrayed all that, and lost the thing worth having, after all. Passive, heroic, he had given himself wholly to his life; but the gift he had owed her, the soldier's one gift, was death; and he had withheld it. He had refused her. And now, at sixty, after all the days, wars, years, countrysides of his life, now he had to turn back and see that he had lost it all, had fought for nothing, that there was no princess in the castle.

1640

Imaginary Countries

"WE CAN'T DRIVE to the river on Sunday," the baron said, "because we're leaving on Friday." The two little ones gazed at him across the breakfast table. Zida said, "Marmalade, please," but Paul, a year older, found in a remote, disused part of his memory a darker dining-room from the windows of which one saw rain falling. "Back to the city?" he asked. His father nodded. And at the nod the sunlit hill outside these windows changed entirely, facing north now instead of south. That day red and yellow ran through the woods like fire, grapes swelled fat on the heavy vines, and the clear, fierce, fenced fields of August stretched themselves out, patient and unboundaried, into the haze of September. Next day Paul knew the moment he woke that it was autumn, and Wednesday. "This is Wednesday," he told Zida, "tomorrow's Thursday, and then Friday when we leave."

"I'm not going to," she replied with indifference, and went off to the Little Woods to work on her unicorn trap. It was made of an egg-crate and many little bits of cloth, with various kinds of bait. She had been making it ever since they found the tracks, and Paul doubted if she would catch even a squirrel in it. He, aware of time and season, ran full speed to the High Cliff to finish the tunnel there before they had to go back to the city.

Inside the house the baroness's voice dipped like a swallow down the attic stairs. "O Rosa! Where *is* the blue trunk then?" And Rosa not answering, she followed her voice, pursuing it and Rosa and the lost trunk down stairs and ever farther hallways to a joyful reunion at the cellar door. Then from his study the baron heard Tomas and the trunk come grunting upward step by step, while Rosa and the baroness began to empty the children's closets, carrying off little loads of shirts and dresses like delicate, methodical thieves. "What are you doing?" Zida asked sternly, having come back for a coat-hanger in which the unicorn might entangle his hoof. "Packing," said the maid. "Not my things," Zida ordered, and departed. Rosa continued rifling her closet. In his study the baron read on undisturbed except by a sense of regret which rose perhaps from the sound of his wife's sweet, distant voice, perhaps from the quality of the sunlight falling across his desk from the uncurtained window.

In another room his older son Stanislas put a microscope, a tennis racket, and a box full of rocks with their labels coming unstuck into his suitcase, then gave it up. A notebook in his pocket, he went down the cool red halls and stairs, out the door into the vast and sudden sunlight of the yard. Josef, reading under the Four Elms, said, "Where are you off to? It's hot." There was no time for stopping and talking. "Back soon," Stanislas replied politely and went on, up the road in dust and sunlight, past the High Cliff where his half-brother Paul was digging. He stopped to survey the engineering. Roads metalled with white clay zigzagged over the cliff-face. The Citroen and the Rolls were parked near a bridge spanning an erosion-gully. A tunnel had been pierced and was in process of enlargement. "Good tunnel," Stanislas said. Radiant and filthy, the engineer replied, "It'll be ready to drive through this evening, you want to come to the ceremony?" Stanislas nodded, and went on. His road led up a long, high hillslope, but he soon turned from it and, leaping the ditch, entered his kingdom and the kingdom of the trees. Within a few steps all dust and bright light were gone. Leaves overhead and underfoot; an air like green water through which birds swam and the dark trunks rose lifting their burdens, their crowns, towards the other element, the sky. Stanislas went first to the Oak and stretched his arms out, straining to reach a quarter of the way around the trunk. His chest and cheek were pressed against the harsh, scored bark; the smell of it and its shelf-fungi and moss was in his nostrils and the darkness of it in his eyes. It was a bigger thing than he could ever hold. It was very old, and alive, and did not know that he was there. Smiling, he went on quietly, a notebook full of maps in his pocket, among the trees towards yet-uncharted regions of his land.

Josef Brone, who had spent the summer assisting his professor with documentation of the history of the Ten Provinces in the Early Middle Ages, sat uneasily reading in the shade of elms. Country wind blew across the pages, across his lips. He looked up from the Latin chronicle of a battle lost nine hundred years ago to the roofs of the house called Asgard. Square as a box, with a sediment of porches, sheds, and stables, and square to the compass, the house stood in its flat yard; after a while in all directions the fields rose up slowly, turning into hills, and behind them were higher hills, and behind them sky. It was like a white box in a blue and yellow bowl, and Josef, fresh from college and intent upon the Jesuit seminary he would enter in the fall, ready to read documents and make abstracts and copy references, had been embarrassed to find that the baron's family called the place after the home of the northern gods. But this no longer troubled him. So much had happened here that he had not expected, and so little seemed to have been finished. The history was years from completion. In three months he had never found out where Stanislas went, alone, up the road. They were leaving on Friday. Now or never. He got up and followed the boy. The road passed a ten-foot bank, half-way up which clung the little boy Paul, digging in the dirt with his fingers, making a noise in his throat: rrrm, rrrrm. A couple of toy cars lay at the foot of the bank. Josef followed the road on up the hill and presently began expecting to reach the top, from which he would see where Stanislas had gone. A farm came into sight and went out of sight, the road climbed, a lark went up singing as if very near the sun; but there was no top. The only way to go downhill on this road was to turn around. He did so. As he neared the woods above Asgard a boy leapt out onto the road, quick as a hawk's shadow. Josef called his name, and they met in the white glare of dust. "Where have you been?" asked Josef, sweating. — "In the Great Woods," Stanislas answered, "that grove there." Behind him the trees gathered thick and dark. "Is it cool in there?" Josef asked wistfully. "What do you do in there?" — "Oh, I map trails. Just for the fun of it. It's bigger than it looks." Stanislas hesitated, then added, "You haven't been in it? You might like to see the Oak." Josef followed him over the ditch and through the close green air to the Oak. It was the biggest tree he had ever seen; he had not seen very many. "I suppose it's very old," he said, looking up puzzled at the reach of branches, galaxy after galaxy of green leaves without end. "Oh, a century or two or three or six," said the boy, "see if you can reach around it!" Josef spread out his arms and strained, trying vainly to keep his cheek off the rough bark. "It takes four men to reach around it," Stanislas said. "I call it Yggdrasil. You know. Only of course Yggdrasil was an ash, not an oak. Want to see Loki's Grove?" The road and the hot white sunlight were gone entirely. The young man followed his guide farther into the maze and game of names which was also a real forest: trees, still air, earth. Under tall grey alders above a dry streambed they discussed the tale of the death of Baldur, and Stanislas pointed out to Josef the dark clots, high in the boughs of lesser oaks, of mistletoe. They left the woods and went down the road towards Asgard. Josef walked along stiffly in the dark suit he had bought for his last year at the University, in his pocket a book in a dead language. Sweat ran down his face, he felt very happy. Though he had no maps and was rather late arriving, at least he had walked once through the forest. They passed Paul still burrowing, ignoring the clang of the iron triangle down at the house, which signalled meals, fires, lost children, and other noteworthy events. "Come on, lunch!" Stanislas ordered. Paul slid down the bank and they proceeded, seven, fourteen and twenty-one, sedately to the house.

That afternoon Josef helped the professor pack books, two

trunks full of books, a small library of medieval history. Josef liked to read books, not pack them. The professor had asked him, not Tomas, "Lend me a hand with the books, will you?" It was not the kind of work he had expected to do here. He sorted and lifted and stowed away load after load of resentment in insatiable iron trunks, while the professor worked with energy and interest, swaddling incunabula like babies, handling each volume with affection and despatch. Kneeling with keys he said, "Thanks, Josef! That's that," and lowering the brass catchbars locked away their summer's work, done with, that's that. Josef had done so much here that he had not expected to do, and now nothing was left to do. Disconsolate, he wandered back to the shade of the elms; but the professor's wife, with whom he had not expected to fall in love, was sitting there. "I stole your chair," she said amiably, "sit on the grass." It was more dirt than grass, but they called it grass, and he obeyed. "Rosa and I are worn out," she said, "and I can't bear to think of tomorrow. It's the worst, the next-to-last day—linens and silver and turning dishes upside down and putting out mousetraps and there's always a doll lost and found after everybody's searched for hours under a pile of laundry—and then sweeping the house and locking it all up. And I hate every bit of it, I hate to close this house." Her voice was light and plaintive as a bird's calling in the woods, careless whether anybody heard its plaintiveness, careless of its plaintiveness. "I hope you've liked it here," she said.

"Very much, baroness."

"I hope so. I know Severin has worked you very hard. And we're so disorganised. We and the children and the visitors, we always seem to scatter so, and only meet in passing. . . . I hope it hasn't been distracting." It was true; all summer in tides and cycles the house had been full or half full of visitors, friends of the children, friends of the baroness, friends, colleagues and neighbors of the baron, duck-hunters who slept in the disused stable since the spare bedrooms were full of Polish medieval historians, ladies with broods of children the smallest of whom fell inevitably into the pond about this time of the afternoon. No wonder it was so still, so autumnal now: the rooms vacant, the pond smooth, the hills empty of dispersing laughter.

"I have enjoyed knowing the children," Josef said, "particularly Stanislas." Then he went red as a beet, for Stanislas alone was not her child. She smiled and said with timidity, "Stanislas is very nice. And fourteen—fourteen is such a fearful age, when you find out so fast what you're capable of being, but also what a toll the world expects. . . . He handles it very gracefully. Paul and Zida now, when they get that age they'll lump through it and be tiresome. But Stanislas learned loss so young. . . . When will you enter the seminary?" she asked, moving from the boy to him in one reach of thought. "Next month," he answered looking down, and she asked, "Then you're quite certain it's the life you want to lead?" After a pause and still not looking at her face, though the white of her dress and the green and gold of leaves above her filled his eyes, he said, "Why do you ask, baroness?"

"Because the idea of celibacy terrifies me," she replied, and he wanted to stretch out on the ground flecked with elm leaves like thin oval coins of gold, and die.

"Sterility," she said, "you see, sterility is what I fear, I dread. It is my enemy. I know we have other enemies, but I hate it most, because it makes life less than death. And its allies are horrible: hunger, sickness, deformation, and perversion, and ambition, and the wish to be secure. What on earth are the children doing down there?" Paul had asked Stanislas at lunch if they could play Ragnarok once more. Stanislas had consented, and so was now a Frost Giant storming with roars the ramparts of Asgard represented by a drainage ditch behind the pond. Odin hurled lightning from the walls, and Thor— "Stanislas!" called the mother rising slender and in white from her chair beside the young man, "don't let Zida use the hammer, please."

"I'm Thor, I'm Thor, I got to have a hammer!" Zida screamed. Stanislas intervened briefly, then made ready to storm the ramparts again, with Zida now at his side, on all fours. "She's Fenris the Wolf now," he called up to the mother, his voice ringing through the hot afternoon with the faintest edge of laughter. Grim and stern, one eye shut, Paul gripped his staff and faced the advancing armies of Hel and the Frozen Lands.

"I'm going to find some lemonade for everybody," the baroness said, and left Josef to sink at last face down on the earth, surrendering to the awful sweetness and anguish she had awakened in him, and would it ever sleep again? while down by the pond Odin strove with the icy army on the sunlit battlements of heaven.

Next day only the walls of the house were left standing. Inside it was only a litter of boxes and open drawers and hurrying people carrying things. Tomas and Zida escaped, he, being slow-witted amid turmoil and the only year-round occupant of Asgard, to clean up the yard out of harm's way, and she to the Little Woods all afternoon. At five Paul shrilled from his window, "The car! The car! It's coming!" An enormous black taxi built in 1923 groaned into the yard, feeling its way, its blind, protruding headlamps flashing in the western sun. Boxes, valises, the blue trunk and the two iron trunks were loaded into it by Tomas, Stanislas, Josef, and the taxi-driver from the village, under the agile and efficient supervision of Baron Severin Egideskar, holder of the Follen Chair of Medieval Studies at the University of Krasnoy. "And you'll get us back together with all this at the station tomorrow at eight— right?" The taxi-driver, who had done so each September for seven years, nodded. The taxi laden with the material impediments of seven people lumbered away, changing gears down the road in the weary, sunny stillness of late afternoon, in which the house stood intact once more room after empty room.

The baron now also escaped. Lighting a pipe he strolled slowly but softly, like one escaping, past the pond and past Tomas's chickencoops, along a fence overgrown with ripe wild grasses bowing their heavy, sunlit heads, down to the grove of weeping birch called the Little Woods. "Zida?" he said, pausing in the faint, hot shade shaken by the ceaseless trilling of crickets in the fields around the grove. No answer. In a cloud of blue pipe-smoke he paused again beside an egg-crate decorated with many little bits of figured cloth and colored paper. On the mossy, much-trodden ground in front of it lay a wooden coat hanger. In one of the compartments of the crate was an eggshell painted gold, in another a bit of quartz, in another a breadcrust. Nearby, a small girl lay sound asleep with her shoes off, her rump higher than her head. The baron sat down on the moss near her, relit his pipe, and contemplated the egg-crate. Presently he tickled the soles of the child's feet. She snorted. When she began to wake, he took her onto his lap.

"What is that?"

"A trap for catching a unicorn." She brushed hair and leafmold off her face and arranged herself more comfortably on him.

"Caught any?"

"No."

"Seen any?"

"Paul and I found some tracks."

"Split-hoofed ones, eh?"

She nodded. Delicately through twilight in the baron's imagination walked their neighbor's young white pig, silver between birch trunks.

"Only young girls can catch them, they say," he murmured, and then they sat still for a long time.

"Time for dinner," he said. "All the tablecloths and knives and forks are packed. How shall we eat?"

"With our fingers!" She leapt up, sprang away. "Shoes," he ordered, and laboriously she fitted her small, cool, dirty feet into leather sandals, and then, shouting "Come on, papa!" was off. Quick and yet reluctant, seeming not to follow and yet never far behind her, he came on between the long vague shadows of the birch trees, along the fence, past the chickencoops and the shining pond, into captivity.

They all sat on the ground under the Four Elms. There was cold ham, pickles, cold fried eggplant with salt, hard bread and hard red wine. Elm leaves like thin coins stuck to the bread. The pure, void, windy sky of after-sunset reflected in the pond and in the wine. Stanislas and Paul had a wrestling match and dirt flew over the remains of the ham; the baroness and Rosa, lamenting, dusted the ham. The boys went off to run cars through the tunnel in High

Cliff, and discuss what ruin the winter rains might cause. For it would rain. All the nine months they were gone from Asgard rain would beat on the roads and hills, and the tunnel would collapse. Stanislas lifted his head a moment thinking of the Oak in winter when he had never seen it, the roots of the tree that upheld the world drinking dark rain underground. Zida rode clear round the house twice on the shoulders of the unicorn, screaming loudly for pure joy, for eating outside on the ground with fingers, for the first star seen (only from the corner of the eye) over the high fields faint in twilight. Screaming louder with rage she was taken to bed by Rosa, and instantly fell asleep. One by one the stars came out, meeting the eye straight on. One by one the young people went to bed. Tomas with the last half-bottle sang long and hoarsely in the Dorian mode in his room above the stable. Only the baron and his wife remained out in the autumn darkness under leaves and stars.

"I don't want to leave," she murmured.

"Nor I."

"Let's send the books and clothes on back to town, and stay here without them. . . ."

"Forever," he said; but they could not. In the observance of season lies order, which was their realm. They sat on for a while longer, close side by side as lovers of twenty; then rising he said, "Come along, it's late, Freya." They went through darkness to the house, and entered.

In coats and hats, everyone ate bread and drank hot milk and coffee out on the porch in the brilliant early morning. "The car! It's coming!" Paul shouted, dropping his bread in the dirt. Grinding and changing gears, headlamps sightlessly flashing, the taxi came, it was there. Zida stared at it, the enemy within the walls, and began to cry. Faithful to the last to the lost cause of summer, she was carried into the taxi head first, screaming, "I won't go! I don't want to go!" Grinding and changing gears the taxi started. Stanislas's head stuck out of the right front window, the baroness's head out of the left rear, and Zida's red, desolate, and furious face was pressed against the oval back window, so that those three saw Tomas waving good-bye under the white walls of Asgard in the sunlight in the bowl of hills. Paul had no access to a window; but he was already thinking of the train. He saw, at the end of the smoke and the shining tracks, the light of candles in a high dark dining-room, the stare of a rockinghorse in an attic corner, leaves wet with rain overhead on the way to school, and a grey street shortened by a cold, foggy dusk through which shone, remote and festive, the first streetlight of December.

But all this happened a long time ago, nearly forty years ago; I do not know if it happens now, even in imaginary countries.

1935